The Fort

The Fort

RP Burke

To order additional copies of this book, contact:
Xlibris
1-888-795-4274
www.Xlibris.com
Orders@Xlibris.com
787042

Dedication

To my father, a man who has always been
worthy of trust and confidence.

Chapter 1

Jack awakened to the sound of his father closing the front door behind him on his way to work. Pulling his New York Yankees blanket off his head, he rubbed his eyes and stretched out his arms, listening to the steady hum of the air-conditioning unit in his bedroom window. Early morning sunlight appeared blurry through the condensation on the window pane above.

Rolling onto his back, Jack reflected that today was the first day of summer vacation. His sixth and final year at Oak Hill Elementary had come to an end, bringing with it ten weeks of summer freedom. He wasn't particularly excited, not because he loved his elementary school, particularly some of his overly strict teachers, but because the thought of having to move to Emerson Middle School revolted him. The facility resembled a decaying prison, with high brick walls, very few windows, and an athletic field surrounded by a chain-link fence and bearing more dusty brown dirt than blades of grass.

Jackson "Jack" O'Malley was small for his age. At four feet eleven inches tall and weighing eighty-two pounds, he was not looking forward to spending two years at Emerson, amongst a group of 7th and 8th graders who were all bigger and stronger than him. His father told him not to worry about his size, "you'll soon hit your growth spurt," but Jack was doubtful, having not met many six-foot men between his six uncles and both of his five-foot-something grandfathers. And the fact that many of his friends from Oak Hill would now be attending a different middle school than him meant having to adjust to being a small kid in a larger school of giant strangers. His mother had tried to explain how school zones determined which school he would attend, but he still couldn't understand why he had to attend Emerson when Brian Sheehan, who only lived four blocks away, got to attend Annandale.

Jack climbed out of bed and went to the kitchen. After picking up the newspaper from the front porch, he poured milk on his bowl of Cheerios and sat down at the dining room table. His parents both believed that he should stay abreast of current events, so he had formed the habit of reading every edition of the *Washington Post*, *Newsweek* magazine, and his favorite, *Sports Illustrated*.

The front section of the newspaper was devoted to Senator Kennedy's funeral, President Johnson working to get a tax increase passed by Congress, and a few stories detailing the ongoing war in Vietnam and related demonstrations across the U.S. Keeping abreast of current events should be accompanied by a session with a psychiatrist, Jack thought wryly to himself as he eagerly moved on to the sports page.

The Yankees had swept a Sunday doubleheader against the Angels, but they were still four games below .500 for the season. With Mickey Mantle only batting .235, it appeared that this would be another tough year for his favorite team, which had not had a winning season in four long years. In Jack's opinion, they never should have traded Roger Maris to St. Louis. It broke up the magic for the team, plus Maris had always been Jack's favorite player. Then again, as he checked the Cardinals box score he saw that Maris' batting average was even lower than Mantle's at .227.

After rinsing out his cereal bowl, Jack got dressed in jeans, a tee shirt, and sneakers. He quickly brushed his teeth, splashed some cold water on his face, and combed his short brown hair. As his mother and his seven-year-old brother Brendan were still asleep, he left a note on the dining room table that read, "I've gone out to play."

It was only 8:00 a.m., but the temperature was already in the eighties and the humid air made him feel as though steam should be rising from the pavement. Seeing no outside movement from his friends' homes across the street, Jack jumped on his bike and began riding around the cul-de-sac. Moving quickly through the warm air helped dry some of the perspiration that had already begun to accumulate on his face.

Jack's family lived in a modest brick home with three bedrooms. It looked similar to the other nine homes on roughly quarter-acre lots along Weeping Willow Court. Many of the families who lived in the Browning Park neighborhood of Annandale, Virginia had children, several whom were his friends. Riding his bike in front of their homes, therefore, was like dangling a worm on a hook in front of a catfish, and within fifteen minutes, Jack was joined by Gary Saunders.

Gary had wavy brown hair and was about three inches taller and ten pounds heavier than Jack, and he had slightly bucked teeth that seemed to grow longer when he was unhappy and his upper lip tightened. His father owned an auto repair business that must have been successful, because Gary seemed to have more cool stuff than Jack did, and his parents owned another small home at a lake about an hour from Annandale. Even though a day never seemed to go by without the two boys getting into a disagreement, and sometimes even worse, they were close. They were just both too competitive, so thought Jack.

"Isn't it great to not be going to school? We should work on building the fort today. I've been collecting pieces of plywood and some two-by-fours left over from the shed my dad built. I've even drawn a picture of how it would look," said Gary in his usual, take-charge manner. "What stuff can you bring, Jack?"

Jack and Gary had been looking forward to building a tree house in the wooded area behind Weeping Willow Court and had named their project The Fort. The woods, as Jack and his friends referred to the undeveloped land, seemed in their minds to be of infinite size. It ran from behind the cul-de-sac on Gary's side of the street to Annandale Road, about a thousand yards from the Saunders' house. From there it continued beyond Browning Park, touching up to adjacent neighborhoods for approximately a mile, thick with an array of trees, bushes, creeks, and wildlife. Large oak, cherry, poplar, chestnut, sycamore, and maple trees shed a splendor of hues through the cracks of sunlight. To Jack, many of these trees appeared to be a hundred feet high, punctuated by stretches of colorful dogwoods, pines, river birch, waves of brush with prickly thorns and leafy strands of vine covered with white honeysuckle flowers. Their parents had restricted Jack and his friends to exploring about a hundred-yard area of the expanse.

"Probably a hammer and maybe some nails. I don't think we have any wood in our basement, but I can check," replied Jack, realizing that he would have to sneak these from his father's workbench because his mother would be worried that he might lose or break the household's only hammer.

"That's OK," smirked Gary, "you can just carry wood and supplies and do some of the manual labor at the site and I will be in charge. Just like my Dad always says, the world needs ditch diggers."

Chapter 2

Jack and Gary gathered behind the Saunders' house near the shed
Gary's father had built. Jack carried his father's hammer and a few
nails of assorted lengths that he managed to find on his father's
basement workbench. Inside the shed, Gary handed him two big
boxes of four-inch penny nails. Then, gathering ten evenly cut,
twenty-four-inch pieces of two-by-fours and placing them inside of a
large burlap sack, he asked Jack to put the nails and his hammer in
the sack with them.

Gary grabbed his own hammer and instructed Jack to lug the
heavy burlap bag as the boys descended the four-foot embankment
separating Gary's backyard from the forest. The smell of damp
leaves, moss, and dogwood blossoms filled the boys' senses as they
entered the woods. Twigs crunched and cracked beneath their
sneakers, alerting the squirrels, rabbits, and other wildlife that they
had company. The weight of the burlap bag that Jack had slung over
his shoulder felt heavier with each step.

"It's your turn to carry the bag," Jack said as he stopped and set
it on the ground.

"Stop complaining, we are almost there. I need to select the perfect tree for our fort," insisted Gary. "Besides, I already did a lot of work, cutting the two-by-fours for us to use as a temporary ladder."

Jack picked the bag back up and continued following Gary, thinking to himself how much he resented the way his friend always bossed him around. Just because Gary's parents had a shed with lumber and all sorts of tools – even an electric circular saw mounted on a table – didn't make him better than Jack. He was already starting to get the feeling that it had been a bad idea to team up with Gary on this project, and the first nail hadn't even been pounded.

Soon Gary stopped and pointed to a large sprawling oak. "Look, this one is perfect."

The tree's trunk extended straight upwards to three times their height, where two large, horizontal branches extended to the left about four feet apart.

"Those will be perfect for the base of our fort," said Gary as he pointed at the two sturdy limbs.

The tree was perfect, Jack had to admit, although he would have preferred Gary ask his opinion before making the decision. The tree was probably sixty yards from the embankment at their back, yet the dense woods made the Saunders' home impossible to spot.

"I guess this will do," Jack muttered.

Gary grabbed the burlap bag and removed the two-by-fours and the nails. "Now we need to nail these blocks of wood to the tree so we can use them as a temporary ladder. Once the fort is finished we can make a rope ladder that can be pulled up to prevent others from getting to the fort while we are in it," he instructed.

Gary set to work, and had nailed the first three boards to the tree before Jack could chime in.

"I think it's my turn to do some hammering," he chirped.

"I'll let you do some in a few minutes, but for now can you just hand me another board?" asked Gary matter-of-factly.

After Gary hammered the next three boards into the tree, Jack told him that he wasn't going to hand him another board unless he got a turn putting up the remaining four pieces. Gary reluctantly climbed down to the ground and handed him the tape measure, which Jack placed in his pocket along with four nails.

Tucking a two-by-four under one arm and the hammer in his other pocket, Jack climbed up the ladder until his feet were on the fourth rung. He placed a nail and the hammer on the sixth ladder step, then pulled out the tape measure to mark a spot above, using his fingernail to scratch the bark on the tree. Now the tricky part was that he would need to use both hands, one to hold the nail to the board against the tree and the other to hold the hammer. Although he was only standing four or five feet off the ground, Jack felt uncomfortable with heights and could feel his nerves starting to kick in.

"Maybe I should have let Gary finish this up, after all," Jack muttered to himself.

Taking a deep breath, he made a quick decision. If he started to fall he would drop the hammer and whatever he was holding to quickly grab one of the ladder steps before he could fall to the ground. This mental plan helped him to relax, giving him enough confidence to swing the hammer and contact the nail. A few swings later, the first nail was firmly through the board and into the tree.

Chapter 3

Once they had finished the temporary ladder, Jack and Gary decided that it was a good time to grab some lunch. Jack declined an invitation to eat at Gary's house because he knew that Mrs. Saunders loved to put mayonnaise on every form of sandwich imaginable. Who ate peanut butter and mayonnaise sandwiches, anyway? Jack disliked the condiment to the point that he would become nearly nauseous watching others eat it in his presence. Instead, he went to his house and made himself a peanut butter and jelly sandwich and poured himself a glass of milk.

Jack's mother emerged from the basement carrying a laundry basket with freshly folded towels. "I have some news for you that I know you're going to love. I spoke on the phone this morning with your Aunt Marcia, and we agreed to have your cousin Elbert come and spend some time with us."

Jack knew that his cousin had been going through a rough time ever since the death of his father in a car accident just three months earlier. Elbert was one year older than Jack, yet he always treated Jack as his equal – almost like a brother.

"That's great, Mom. When will he be here?"

"Aunt Marcia is putting him on a Greyhound bus in Clarksburg Friday morning, and he should arrive here in time for supper. I think we should pick him up at the bus station in Springfield at 4:30. We'll need to bring the extra mattress down from the attic and put it in your bedroom for him to use, although his feet will probably dangle off the edge. Marcia said that boy is nearly six feet tall!"

Elbert Thaddeus Justice, III, was unlike anyone Jack had ever met. He had always been a giant among his classmates, having inherited his size and strength from his father, Elbert Justice, Jr. Uncle Bert had been a rugged outdoorsman, six foot four inches and about 220 pounds of solid muscle. As an engineer and scientist, he had earned his PhD from Virginia Tech when he was only twenty-five years old, and later developed a research lab and consulting firm that specialized in working with glass particles used in products such as fiberglass insulation.

Uncle Bert had been warm but reserved, soft-spoken, thoughtful, and always precise in his word choice. Jack's father always said that he was probably the most intelligent person he'd ever met – and to Jack, Elbert seemed to have inherited that trait from his father as well. Jack recalled how quiet Elbert had seemed when they attended his father's funeral in Clarksburg, West Virginia. He'd hardly cried at all, but his stare was blank and he hardly spoke a word.

As an only child, Elbert had been very close with his father, who had taught him how to hunt and fish on their frequent camping trips along the West Fork River, where they had also included time for rock climbing and kayaking. But Elbert resisted his parents' attempts to nickname him Bert or Thad, and insisted on using the birth name of his now-deceased grandfather. A decorated war hero in World War I after enlisting in the Army at only seventeen years of age, he later graduated from West Virginia University with a degree in business and later founded Justice Glass, a large manufacturer of glass products that at one time had become one of the largest manufacturers of colored glass products in the nation, employing nearly one-tenth of the population of Clarksburg.

"As things stand now, Elbert should be with us for about a month, but as you know he's been quiet and sad since Uncle Bert died, so we'll just have to see how things go while he's here. Aunt Marcia hopes that by getting away and hanging out with you, he'll be able to get back to being his old self," Jack's mother said.

"I'm sure he'll have a good time here, Mom," said Jack. "Gary and I are building a tree fort in the woods, and knowing Elbert, he'll love exploring back there."

"Speaking of you and Gary…" his mother asked as she raised her eyebrows, "how are you two getting along?"

"Well I haven't hit him with a two-by-four yet, but he does sort of treat me like his unpaid laborer," said Jack.

"Well try to have fun together and resist the urge to argue or fight. If he gets on your nerves, just leave and find some other friends to play with. I have some more laundry to work on and then I need to pick your brother up from swim practice. Just be sure to be home in time for dinner," she said as she picked the laundry basket up and left the room.

Jack's parents had inexpensively acquired a membership at the Kenworth Recreational Pool to give their boys a place to go swimming and socialize with their friends, and Brendan had been taking lessons twice each week. He was making rapid improvements, and the lifeguard had convinced him that he should join the swim team. Yet in reality, the team for seven-to-eight-year-olds was short on swimmers, and Brendan's recruitment to the team was more a matter of necessity to help field a team than it was a matter of his natural-born talent.

Gary was still finishing his lunch, so Jack jumped on his bike and circled the cul-de-sac. Soon, he noticed Dana Allen, who lived next door to Gary. Dana was the youngest of the three Allen sisters and, having grown up with mostly boys in the neighborhood, had developed into a tomboy. She could run as fast as and out-wrestle any of the boys on the block.

With her blond hair pulled into a ponytail, she was kneeling near a tree in her front yard, barefoot, wearing a pair of white cut-off jean shorts and a bright orange tee shirt. She placed her index finger against her lips, requesting quiet, and waved for Jack to join her.

Jack parked his bike and approached, quietly kneeling next to her on the front lawn. She held a string tied to a small stick, which held up one side of an upside-down cigar box, laid on the ground about twenty feet away, near a group of trees in the Allens' yard. The lid of the cigar box rested flat beneath the trap, and on it were a few almonds and blueberries.

"Do you see that chipmunk near the tree?" whispered Dana.

Sure enough, Jack saw a chipmunk near the box, scampering close to survey the food before periodically running away. Suddenly the chipmunk made its move for one of the nuts and Dana yanked on the string. But as the stick was yanked away, its edge grabbed the box, flipping it over with the chipmunk and the nuts and the berries so that all three were inside with the lid wide open.

Dana stood to run towards the box, but the chipmunk quickly jumped out, an almond firmly in its mouth, and fled the scene through a row of hedges at the edge of the yard.

Dana and Jack turned to hear loud laughter coming from behind them. It was Gary.

"Way to go, Dana! That chipmunk's a lot smarter than you, but I'm sure he's grateful for the lunch. If you wanted your trap to work you should have asked me to help you, because I never would have used a stick with a rough edge that could catch on the box. I would have used a popsicle stick with a rounded edge."

Dana's face turned red. "Shut up, Gary, or I'll knock those two buck-teeth of yours down your throat."

Gary ignored her comment. "That's fine. I was going to invite you to help me and Jack build our fort in the woods, but since you're being such a jerk, you can stay here in your yard and feed more of the wildlife with your stupid box."

"You don't get to decide if Dana can help all by yourself Gary," insisted Jack.

"Don't worry, Jack. I don't want anything to do with Gary or his stupid fort. And come to think of it, Gary...that chipmunk's teeth looked a lot like yours," Dana said as she walked away.

Chapter 4

Gary used his father's circular saw to cut five two-by-fours of approximately three to four feet in length. They would use these as the base for their fort. After placing the wood, nails, hammer, and a long rope in the burlap bag, the boys headed back to the woods with Jack again carrying the bag.

At the site, Gary climbed out on one of the branches and pulled out the rope. He tied one end around the branch he was seated on, fixing it with a double knot and dropping the other end to the ground. He pulled two nails from his pocket and hammered them into the trunk of the tree to serve as a hook, allowing him to hang the hammer and free up his hands.

Then Jack tied the rope to one of the two-by-fours, allowing Gary to pull it up into the tree. He then extended the board so it rested on top of the slightly lower branch and pounded two nails into the board, making certain it was firmly fastened into the branch. He then slid out further on the branch and continued to hammer nails, turning the board into a brace for the branch.

After hammering a similar board to the slightly higher branch, he fastened two more boards across the two branches at the ends of the first two boards, creating a square foundation. With the four boards now firmly connecting the two branches, the plywood floor was ready to be added in their next phase of construction.

Back in the shed, Gary cut two, six-by-two sheets of plywood, which when laid side by side would make up the floor for the fort. They each carried a piece down to the tree, complaining about the weight of the wood and its coarse edges as it cut into their fingers. Each piece of plywood weighed more than twenty pounds, making it impossible for either boy to simply lift into the tree by himself. With a rope in his pocket, Jack climbed the tree, tied a double knot around one of the branches, and lowered the second rope to the ground.

Gary then tied both ropes around one piece of plywood and climbed into the tree, and with each boy pulling at the same time they were soon able to lift the plywood up to the branch and place it across the foundation. Repeating the process with the second board and making sure that both pieces of plywood were connected tightly together, Gary nailed the floor to the four two-by-fours beneath.

Jack and Gary lay on their backs on the freshly laid floor of their fort to gaze into the leaves and branches of the oak above them, a sense of satisfaction filling them both as they took in the fresh air, the sounds of the forest, and the streaks of sunlight breaking through the trees.

"Do you see the nest in that branch up to the left?" asked Gary. "Imagine how many trips the bird must have made back and forth to build its fort?"

"Maybe the bird had another bird to be its laborer…doing most of the carrying while it did the supervising?" joked Jack.

The boys returned to the shed, where Gary filled the burlap sack with more two-by-fours that Gary had measured and cut to build the frame for the fort. He instructed Jack to carry it to the fort while he finished cutting the remaining plywood, and before long the fort had a solid floor, a frame, and a roof. Now all it needed were walls, a cover for the roof, and tape to cover up cracks in the joints. As they finished for the day, Jack asked Gary more directly why he hadn't allowed him to hammer a single nail all day.

"You complain too much" started Gary. "I know a lot of people who would gladly work with me if you don't want to help. The supplies have been coming from me, not you. The design and the tools are all mine, not yours. If you don't want to help, then don't, but please stop whining about it. You're lucky I'm even letting you work with me."

Jack realized that Gary was right about him not providing any of the supplies or tools. But Gary's father was the one providing these – not Gary. Without responding, Jack simply turned to walk home.

"So are you going to come back and help tomorrow?" Gary yelled after him.

Jack continued walking, ignoring the question.

At home, Jack found Brendan and his friend Bruce kneeling on the front walkway, looking down at the concrete and giggling at something.

"What are you two up to?" asked Jack.

"We're drowning ants," replied Brendan. He spit, targeting a pair of unsuspecting ants as each went about its business. The glob of saliva clung to their bodies like quicksand.

"Sounds like fun," Jack said, shaking his head as he walked towards the garden hose at the side of the house. Turning the nozzle, Jack took several gulps of cool water squirting from the end of the hose. He then pulled the hose to the front of the house. Placing his thumb over the tip, he sprayed water at Brendan and Bruce, causing them to jump up and run away to escape the spray.

"I'm telling Mom," cried Brendan as he and Bruce stared at Jack from a distance.

"Now you know what it's like to be an ant!" Jack replied as he returned the hose and shut off the faucet.

Chapter 5

Jack was small for his age, but he had long felt that he had one quality that made him special: his self-discipline. If there was anything that he felt was important to him, he always seemed to be able to muster the sometimes boring and monotonous consistency to stick to an activity, well after most of his friends had lost interest.

None of them read the daily newspaper from front to back the way Jack did. Nor did any read *Newsweek* religiously. Some did read *Sports Illustrated*, but few seemed to know how to calculate batting averages and earned run averages as quickly or as accurately as Jack.

Jack's interest in politics especially impressed his teachers. When Jack was in the third grade, his teacher Mrs. Clayton asked him to give a report to the class on the outcome of the 1964 Presidential election. Jack had begged and pleaded with his parents until they relented to let him watch the televised news broadcast of the election until it was completed, long after his mother and father had gone to bed for the night. Mrs. Clayton was impressed when Jack reported the advantages Johnson had claimed in the Electoral College and popular vote over his opponent Barry Goldwater, and even she had been unaware that his landslide victory was the largest in popular vote percentage since James Monroe's victory in 1820.

Jack's interest in politics even extended into Congressional races across the country. Using a *Newsweek* article that listed every House of Representatives and Senate race for the year, Jack waited for updates from each state to see who had been declared the winner and placed a checkmark by the candidate who prevailed in the magazine.

When Jack reported that both the House and the Senate would net gains for the Democratic party and give them substantial party majorities over the previously elected Congress, he explained why that would likely make things easier for President Johnson to move forward on his legislative agenda.

In his scorekeeping of the election results, Jack had become familiar with all the Senate candidates who ran for office and with many of the individual candidates for the House. After a couple of election outcomes, he became disappointed whenever a favorite failed to win, almost as if Whitey Ford had lost a tough outing for the Yankees in the World Series. In other races, he was elated, or at least satisfied that he'd correctly predicted how the vote would pan out.

Another area of discipline he had begun to develop was physical training. Each evening, either before or after dinner, he would go into his bedroom and complete three sets of twenty-five push-ups, alternating with three sets of twenty-five sit-ups. He would also do three sets of twenty curl repetitions with ten-pound dumbbells, and three sets of twenty overhead presses. He then ran wind sprints along the half-mile stretch from his house to the next neighborhood and back.

Jack recorded each day's exercise results in a spiral-bound notebook that he kept in the small desk in his room. He took great satisfaction in knowing that he had been making improvements in each of these activities ever since. Encouraged by his physical education instructor, Mr. Janzen, he had begun this process about nine months earlier. Sticking to this regimen five days a week, he had increased his pushups from ten reps per set to twenty-five and his sit-ups from two to three sets. And his mile time had dropped from over nine minutes to less than eight.

Jack completed his entry into the spiral notebook and then went out to the cul-de-sac to see who might want to play a game of kick the can. Dana was sitting on the curb in front of her house with Judy Morrison, a short, twelve-year-old brunette who lived in the corner house at the end of the street.

"If I can round up a few more, are you two up for a game of kick the can?" asked Jack.

"I don't want to get dirty and sweaty," replied Judy, who could never be confused with a tomboy. Judy wore blue jeans, a green and white-striped tee shirt, and white tennis shoes adorned with pink shoelaces. Most days she wore dresses with sandals, even when most of the other twelve-year-old girls were wearing shorts or jeans.

"Come on, Judy, a little dirt won't hurt you, and you're already starting to sweat with it being so humid," pleaded Dana.

With Dana's encouragement working on Judy, Jack ran to Gary's house and then to Kenny Tucker's place next door. Within a few minutes Gary and Kenny had joined the others in the cul-de-sac. Kenny's ten-year-old brother Bobby, a husky boy who wore thick black-framed glasses that often were covered partially by his curly red hair, came out too.

The kids played a modified form of kick the can that centered on the telephone pole at the curb in front of the Tuckers' yard. Gary volunteered to be "it" first and turned to the telephone pole. Closing his eyes, he counted loudly to twenty.

"Here I come!" he shouted, and he ventured a few steps to look through the hedges that surrounded his front yard.

Jack, who liked to keep moving during the game, had run completely around Dana's house before crawling behind the Allens' Ford station wagon parked in the street. So when Gary spied some movement from Judy and Dana in his front yard behind the hedges and ran behind them, Jack saw his opportunity to make a run for the telephone pole and took off from behind the car – but he arrived a few seconds after Gary had thrown the red ball the kids used to tag one another at Dana. Dana quickly rolled on the ground, avoiding the ball, but unfortunately for Judy the ball caught her in the leg just before Jack touched the pole.

"Ha," laughed Gary loudly. "Judy's *it*."

"You're lucky you hit her, Gary," remarked Dana, "because you throw like a girl and you missed me by a mile." She and the others came out to the telephone pole for the next round to begin.

"Shut up, Dana. I was throwing at Judy the whole time and hit her perfectly," lied Gary.

Judy took her turn counting to twenty and yelled, "Ready or not, here I come."

Dana joined Jack as they hid behind bushes in the Tuckers' front yard. Judy was reluctant to venture far from the telephone pole, so those hiding were hesitant to make any moves

As they lay in the grass, Dana whispered to Jack, "Have you ever kissed a girl?"

Jack had always thought that Dana liked him. She was cute, and he liked that she was a tomboy who could run and fight as well as any of his guy friends. He often wondered what it would be like to kiss her, but had never had the courage to cross that line.

"Yes, I've kissed Barbara Bates and Mary Lou Thompkins," replied Jack as he looked at Dana.

"Every boy has kissed Mary Lou Thompkins," said Dana. "But have you ever wanted to kiss me?"

While Jack thought about what that might be like, Dana glanced over his shoulder. Her eyes grew large when she saw Judy approaching. Judy tossed the ball at Jack and easily hit him in the back.

"I got Jack. He's *it!*" yelled Judy as she and the others all returned to the telephone pole.

Chapter 6

The next day the skies were filled with thick clouds and steady rainfall.

Gary called Jack, telling him that due to the weather he was canceling plans to work on the fort, but he invited Jack to come by at 10 a.m. to play a game of Monopoly. Jack's mother often used housework to keep her boys busy on rainy days, and after Jack finished reading the newspaper, his mother asked him to vacuum his room and help his brother move a dresser in his room so he could vacuum the carpet beneath. Then she asked Jack to help her with some ironing. Since he was seven Jack had known how much starch to spray on his father's dress shirts, and how to use the right temperature and steam to make each shirt look crisp before hanging them.

After Jack finished the third shirt, his mother said, "That's enough ironing. I know you want to read the *Newsweek* magazine that arrived yesterday. I'll be back right after I drop off Brendan at swim practice." She paused as she picked up her umbrella. "I guess swimming is one sport that rain doesn't cancel. And by the way, don't forget to call Coach Russell and see if he can give you a ride to baseball practice, if it isn't cancelled today."

Jack called Coach Russell at the small sporting goods store he owned and ran in Annandale. Coach Russell told him to be at his house at 3:30 and he would give him a ride. Jack then sat down and began reading each article in the latest issue of *Newsweek*.

The cover showed Senator Robert Kennedy standing before a large painting of President John Kennedy. The issue had over twenty pages, packed with photographs of the senator, along with images of his family and brother Ted, who gave an emotional eulogy during Robert's funeral service.

Jack remembered watching news coverage of Bobby Kennedy's Presidential primary victory in California shortly before it was announced that he had been shot. In the twenty-six hours from the shooting until his death, Jack prayed for some sort of miracle that would enable the senator to recover. The assassinations of President Kennedy, his brother, and Dr. Martin Luther King were dark and profound experiences for Jack. Their families had been victimized and devastated. Their causes had been abandoned in their void. All three represented the best of America's leaders, debatably still in their early formation, yet all were stolen away by individuals who'd never made a worthwhile contribution to society in any significant fashion. Robert Kennedy might not have won the Democratic nomination, given the large gap to make up between him and Vice President Humphrey, but to have it end this way truly saddened Jack.

The game of Monopoly at Gary's house turned into a disaster. Kenny Tucker and Dana joined Jack in Gary's basement recreation room, which was lined with pine-stained walls and thick beige wall-to-wall carpeting. The large room contained an entertainment center on one end that included a twenty-four-inch black and white television and a phonograph with two large speakers built into the cabinetry. A long plaid sofa and two leather reclining chairs faced the television, while a felt-covered card table with four chairs sat at the opposite end of the room near a wall of bookshelves crammed with volumes of *Reader's Digest* that Mrs. Saunders had been collecting for years.

Before the game began, Gary made it clear to the group that he would be "the banker," responsible for dispensing and collecting monies and serving as the game's arbiter in the event of any rules disputes. He made this pronouncement without the slightest inclination of concern as to how the others felt about his decision.

"That's very democratic of you," Jack said with a sarcastic smirk on his face.

The proceedings went downhill in a hurry when Kenny and Gary started arguing over who would get to use the race car as their game piece and who would end up with the thimble. Kenny thought they should each roll a die to determine who would get the car, but Gary simply informed him that "I'm the banker and you need to listen to what I say."

Kenny was a small, quiet, and nervous boy, with blonde hair in a crew cut. Not wanting to start a fight, he relented, accepting the thimble and shaking his head while chewing on his fingernail.

The rocky proceedings came to a tumultuous halt when, after dispensing each player's initial play dollars, Gary announced, "As the banker, I get to go first and then each of you will take your turns, clockwise from me."

"You're full of crap!" shouted Dana. "Take your game and your banker role and shove them where the sun don't shine." Standing from her seat, she flipped the game board into Gary's lap. Game pieces and Monopoly money sailed towards his shocked and frozen body.

Gary grabbed Dana's hands and stood as he tried to restrain her, but before he knew it, she had shaken loose from his grip and quickly pushed him backwards, knocking him and his chair onto the floor. Mrs. Saunders, having heard the commotion, quickly rushed into the room.

"That's no way to behave in this house, young lady," she shouted at Dana. "Now all of you march yourselves out of this house at once."

As they walked up the basement stairs to leave, the three overheard Gary tell his mother as he lifted himself from the floor, "I have no idea why she got upset, Mom. She's always been a hothead and a bad loser."

Chapter 7

Jack rode to practice with Coach Russell and his son Randy, who played second base, in Mr. Russell's weathered gray Ford pickup, which he'd probably owned for a decade. The coach loved to smoke a cigar with the windows rolled down while he drove to and from practice, often switching to Red-Man chewing tobacco once he made it to the ballpark. Annandale Recreational Park had recently opened to the public boasting three baseball diamonds, each with dugouts and bleachers. The park also featured a concession stand that sold hot dogs and snacks during big games, a picnic area with tables and seating that could handle a group of a hundred or more, and a two-mile nature trail that was popularly frequented by walkers and joggers of all ages.

After Mr. Russell parked in the lot, Jack and Randy each grabbed a canvas bag from the flatbed, one with bats and balls and the other with batting helmets and catcher's equipment.

"Take the equipment over to field number three and I'll be with you in a minute," said Coach, as he put a fresh wad of tobacco into his mouth. He then grabbed a small cooler containing a couple of cold Schaefer beers on ice, brought on account that the damn dusty field always made his throat dry.

After a ten-minute warmup, the players took turns at batting practice for forty-five minutes, with Coach Russell pitching from the mound. The next thirty minutes were devoted to "fungo" practice, in which each player assumed his position in the field, Coach hit fly balls, line drives, or grounders to each position, and the fielders threw the ball back to designated recipients. Base running and situational play took up the final half hour of practice, teaching players how to react when real game-time circumstances warranted.

Jack always played right field because it was the position his favorite player, Roger Maris, played with the Yankees. It was also the only position Coach would allow him to play, because it was generally the spot relegated to the most inept defender. Jack had been born with a lazy eye, and although surgery at age two had corrected the crossed eyes he'd been born with, vision in his left eye never improved beyond 20/200. With his entire line of sight all coming from one eye, Jack's depth perception was off just enough to make it difficult for him to judge fly balls. During fungo practice, Jack performed much better than in real games, because he knew the ball was coming to him – whereas in a game, there was no telling which part of the field the ball may be headed.

While his ability to catch was shaky, Jack did have a strong throwing arm, and Coach Russell yelled, "Nice throw O'Malley" when he fired a perfect throw to the catcher after the last line drive. Jack had also been making improvements with his hitting. He wasn't sure if the improvement had anything to do with his weight training or his running, but he felt that there likely was a connection. As a hitter, he'd always been able to make contact with a fastball, but now that some of the pitchers were learning to throw a curve, he was having trouble staying in the box whenever the ball appeared to be coming towards his body. Jack would react nervously in those situations by bailing away from the plate and away from the ball.

To help Jack overcome his fear of the curve, Coach Russell had been working with him, convincing him to relax and concentrate on the ball as it was released from the pitcher's hand. "Look for the bull's-eye," he would yell to Jack, imploring him to concentrate closely on the ball until the spin of a curve made the red stitching on the baseball appear like a circle or bull's-eye. Jack never could see the bull's-eye, but he did believe that the technique was allowing him to relax a little, mainly because he was more focused on the ball's rotation and not simply on whether the ball might hit him.

As they rode back in the truck after practice, Randy said, "You know Jack, you actually made contact with a couple of the curves Dad threw you today, and you absolutely smashed that one fastball against the fence in center field."

"And I noticed during the wind sprints that you were running faster than anyone on the team," added Coach Russell.

Jack's daily running was starting to pay dividends, and it was nice to know that it was even beginning to show up on his coach's radar. "Thanks for the observations. I really think that this is our year to win the league championship," he said.

Later that evening Jack scarfed down his dinner of meatloaf with mashed potatoes and gravy and green beans. Jack's father watched him devour his food, warning, "You might want to try chewing a little before swallowing."

"Practice went well today, and it sure did make me hungry. Coach Russell said I was doing better on my wind sprints, so I think these nightly runs are beginning to have an impact. I should get in my run before it gets too dark outside," said Jack with a sense of pride.

Jack's Mom smiled. "Well I'm glad to hear that practice went so well, because you have a big game on Monday evening. The Cardinals and the Pirates seem to be fighting it out for the league championship. I know that your cousin will love watching you play against your biggest rival."

"And I found out today that I'll be able go to your game because my trip to New York was postponed. Elbert and your Mom and Brendan and me will all be there," added Mr. O'Malley.

"Cheering you on!" said Mrs. O'Malley.

"I'll be booing you on," teased Brendan as he stuck out his tongue.

Jack was happy to hear that his dad was going to be able to attend. John Thomas O'Malley, or Jack, as his friends called him, worked as a special agent with the U.S. Secret Service. After Senator Kennedy's assassination, Congress had passed legislation to provide Secret Service protection to all major presidential candidates, and Jack Sr. was currently assigned to a special protection detail for several of them who were currently campaigning. Even though the primary elections had already concluded, party caucuses were now in full swing, so every candidate who had enough funds in their campaign accounts wanted to be in those caucus states, shaking hands and kissing babies.

Broader protection was placing an incredible strain on the manpower of the Secret Service. Jack's dad was now working with a team of people "borrowed" from other federal agencies to help manage the expanded list of candidates. It would take time for the Service to hire enough agents to become adequately staffed, and until then, Mr. O'Malley would be on the road more than he would be home.

One of the benefits of being the son of a Secret Service agent, however, was being able to learn more about the people who they protected than the average person could. Mr. O'Malley would never discuss confidential information with his family, but learning about how a candidate treated his staff or interacted with his family often helped Jack to place a politician into the "Good Guy" or "Jerk" column of his political notebook. Fortunately, most were "Good Guys," and no doubt it was these types of conversations with his dad that had inspired Jack's strong interest in politics.

"I talked to Greg McMillian and Bobby Bettman about going to the pool tomorrow, if that's OK, Mom? I think I need to take a break from Gary and his tree fort and I haven't been to the pool in a while," said Jack.

"It's OK with me, as long as you take Brendan with you," Mrs. O'Malley responded. "That way I can run some errands and get ready for Elbert's arrival on Friday. And first thing tomorrow, you need to help me carry the mattress from the attic into your room, and I'll need you to help put sheets and pillow cases on."

With his tongue in his cheek, Jack said, "I'm fine with those conditions, Mom, *even the part about bringing Brendan.* I sure can't wait to have him show me what he's learned from his lessons and swim practice."

"I can swim with my face in the water from one end of the pool to the other now, and I've learned how to breathe by just turning my head to the side every few strokes. I bet I could beat you in a race. But I think I'll invite Bruce too, because I sure won't want to be stuck with you and Greg and Bobby all day," Brendan said, and he stuck out his tongue once more.

Chapter 8

On Thursday, Jack and Brendan finished their chores and headed off to the pool. When he saw his little brother swim two lengths of the Olympic-sized pool freestyle, Jack had to admit that Brendan had really made a lot of improvement. A year ago, he would have not been able to swim even one complete length. After the boys had practiced doing flips off the diving boards and swimming for a few hours, they ordered hot dogs and Cokes from the concession stand and sat in a shaded area where picnic tables had been positioned near the basketball court. They debated who was the best swimmer and who could do the best flip off of the high diving board, and who was the best hitter on their baseball team. Bobby even strayed to the subject of which of the twin Talbot sisters, who were wearing identical floral bathing suits, was better looking, and panic ensued when Anna and Danielle actually started approaching.

"Hi Jack," they said in unison, flashing Jack a smile.

As they moved past and glanced at Bobby and Greg, Anna added, "What are you two staring at?"

As the girls walked away, Jack couldn't resist shaking his head and laughing at his friends. "You two were busted!"

Later that evening, Gary, Dana, and Kenny were circling the cul-de-sac on their bikes while Jack sat on the curb and watched lightening bugs flickering near the trees in Dana's yard. In the backyard of the house to the right of Dana's, he could hear a radio broadcasting the Washington Senators ballgame, and found himself walking towards the source of the broadcast to see if he could catch the score.

"Hi Mr. Atkins," Jack said as he approached.

"Ha! Now Jack O'Malley, how many times have I told you never to call me Mr. Atkins? That's my father's name, God rest his soul. You should call me Nelly," he said with his deep booming voice and a warm smile. Can you believe the Senators are actually leading the Yankees in the bottom of the fourth, one-zero? Hannan is pitching a solid game, but then again, the Yankees aren't the team that they used to be. But don't worry Jack - I know you still love the Yankees, and if I know my Senators they'll figure out a way to blow the lead before the game is over."

"Is Mantle playing?" asked Jack.

"Yes, but Hannan hasn't given him anything to hit, so he's walked both times he's been at the plate," responded Nelly. "Ha! C'mon, Jackson, have a seat and join me for an inning."

Jack sat in the green and white-laced lawn chair beside Nelly's transistor radio, where a mug of coffee, a large ashtray, a flashlight, and a ballpoint pen with a pad of paper were all crowded on a little plastic table. Nelly sat on the other side of the table, a brown blanket beneath him for comfort and his feet up on an old milk crate as if it were an ottoman.

Darnell "Nelly" Atkins had recently retired on disability from his job as a postal worker. Before that, he had had a twenty-year career in the U.S. Army, serving in both France and Germany during World War II. Jack was sure that Nelly, at 5'10" and 250 pounds, was certainly testing the strength of his lawn chair. Clean shaven and sporting a buzz cut of thick white hair, the sixty-one-year-old was built like a cannonball. His meaty forearms were both adorned with tattoos displaying a pair of dice, the numerals six and three showing on each.

Nelly smoked Camel cigarettes like his life depended on it. He suffered from arthritis, particularly in his knees and ankles. He could still move around reasonably well, but whenever he stood up quickly, the pain from his legs would shoot up to his spine and require him to pause a few moments to regain his calm and momentum so he could walk. He and his wife Dee, a lovely southern belle and former homecoming queen with short brown hair and an ever-present smile, took great pride in their lawn and their home, and Jack always felt that because they never had any children, they treated all of the kids on the street like their own.

As the top of the fifth inning ended, Nelly grabbed his coffee mug and tossed its contents into the lawn. "Hey Jack, while the commercial is playing, would you mind running over to the shed and grabbing me a beer. Pour it in the coffee mug and bring it back to me. I'd do it myself, but I'd miss the next inning with these damn legs of mine. And grab a soda for yourself while you're at it."

Jack grabbed the mug to do as he was told. Inside the shed, he found the refrigerator filled with two rows of Ballantine Beer, all in bottles, two rows of soft drinks, and a few bottles of tonic water. He opened a bottle of beer using an opener that was attached to the refrigerator, rinsed the mug, and put the empty bottle in a crate once he'd poured its contents. He admired the orderliness of the shed. Its workbench, tools, and lawn equipment all seemed to be spotless, everything neatly in its place.

After Jack returned and handed him the mug, Nelly smiled. "Ha, that's my boy. So tell me, what big plans do you have for the summer, Jack?"

Jack swallowed his sip of cola before answering. "My cousin Elbert is coming to visit from West Virginia. He should be with us for about a month."

Just then, the light on the back porch turned on as Mrs. Atkins stepped out on the top step. Petite at 5'2" tall, Dee's stature stood in stark contrast to her husband, whom she loved but never let it prevent her from teasing him. She tolerated the baseball her husband listened to as long as she was always able to watch the Dick Van Dyke show, her favorite, and tend to the her rose bushes and azaleas.

"Well hello, Jack O'Malley – I thought I heard voices out here, and figured it was just Nelly talking to himself again," smiled Dee.

"Hi, Mrs. Atkins," replied Jack.

"We're just out here seeing if the Senators will blow another lead, and I'm relaxing and enjoying my *coffee*," added Nelly, with his back to his wife, as he raised his mug and winked at Jack.

"Now Jack, honey, when are you going to learn that you need to start calling me Dee?" She paused and added, "I hope you're both enjoying the ballgame."

She turned off the back porch light, but paused before turning back to the house. "Oh and one last thing, Jack dear," she said, winking at Jack for emphasis, "Please don't let that old con man talk you into fetching him any of his Ballantine beers from that shed of his. Do you understand what I'm saying, sweetie?"

Jack smiled at Mr. Atkins, who was wearing a guilty smirk on his face and whispered to him, "Busted!"

Chapter 9

Marcia Justice stood outside of the bus station and handed her only child a bus ticket and four five-dollar bills. Her son stood a solid seven inches taller than her, and she reached to give him a long embrace.

"I sure am going to miss you," she said. "Make sure to call me as soon as you get to Aunt Kathleen's and remember, I expect you to mind your manners while you are their guest."

"I know. I promise I will," said Elbert as he watched his suitcase being loaded into the luggage compartment of the bus.

"Honey, I know how sad you've been since your father passed away," she said, pausing to fight her own tears, "and Lord knows, I'm not doing any better. But we both need to try to regain our smiles and our energy, so I want you to try to smile a little more while you're away. You know that's what your Daddy would have wanted."

"I'll try, I promise," was the best that he could offer. He turned and climbed the stairs and found a window seat near the middle of the bus. With less than twenty passengers on board, he was pleased to know that he would have the seat beside him empty to stretch out or set down the book and notepad that he'd brought along for the trip.

The bus had a musty smell, probably a result of spilled drinks on the seats and carpeting, and from the cleaning fluids that the maintenance staff used to try to keep them clean. A brunette mother who appeared to be a few years younger than his mom seated two of her three young children in the row just behind his. She made sure that each child was given coloring books and crayons to keep their minds occupied for at least a portion of the nine-hour trip.

As the bus exited the parking lot, Elbert waved to his mother, who refused to leave until the bus was out of sight. He knew that his mom would worry about him until he called to tell her that he had safely arrived. It bothered Elbert that his mother worried so much about the grief that he'd been feeling. And he knew that Uncle Jack and Aunt Kathleen had been warned that he was still sad and fragile, which would probably mean that they would be different with him, walking on eggshells, and not treat him the way they normally would.

What bothered Elbert most was that he couldn't figure out how to be happy and energetic. He didn't know how to communicate his feelings other than to say that when his dad died, so did the old Elbert. He couldn't see a way that he'd ever feel as safe, secure, or happy without his best friend in the world nearby. Why, he bemoaned, couldn't everyone understand that he wouldn't ever be the way he used to be, because a big part of him had departed and nothing was ever going to take the sadness away?

He hoped that his mother was right, that by spending some time with Jack he might regain some of his enthusiasm and energy. He always enjoyed being with Jack because he seemed to understand him better than almost anyone and he accepted him the way that he was. He also liked Jack because he wasn't full of crap like a lot of his friends in West Virginia. He always came across as humble and honest.

The last time that he saw Jack was at his father's funeral, and it had seemed that Jack was the only person at the service or at the gathering at their home who didn't expect anything of him. Most people wanted to hear him say that it would be tough, but he and his mom would get through it – life went on. But Elbert wasn't in the mood to make that concession and frankly, things hadn't changed since that day. Only Jack didn't need any assurances. In fact, he seemed like he could read his mind and was content to simply sit beside him with very little communication, almost as a dog would sit next to his master, wanting to protect him from any danger.

Today was the ninety-fifth day since his father died. He wondered if there would ever come a time when he would stop counting the days he'd outlived his dad. His memory could not seem to stop replaying the words, "I'm sorry, there has been a terrible accident," that the police officer said to him and his mother on that fateful evening.

Elbert could not accept the fact that his father had suddenly swerved his vehicle off the highway, destroying the guard rail and rolling his truck down a sharp embankment, flipping numerous times and violently smashing into a tree. His mind couldn't reconcile the safe driving skills that his father had always exhibited with the police inspection report that estimated he must have been traveling at nearly ninety miles per hour before swerving to miss something, perhaps a deer, and then losing control and launching the truck down the embankment. His dad knew that highway like the back of his hand, having driven that route between Clarksburg and Morgantown weekly to teach a graduate class in engineering.

Elbert closed his eyes, trying to stop the vision from replaying. He forced his mind to pull up the image of the time last September when he and his dad went trout fishing in a stream on the Cranberry River. It had been a cool overcast day and he recalled how his father's eyes seemed to beam in pride as he watched Elbert hook a twenty-inch brook trout after a strong fight lasting nearly ninety seconds. "That's the largest trout we're going to catch in this shallow stream, son. I think that streamer we made appears to be a winner," he had said as he carefully removed the handmade fly and released the trout back into the stream. This was the image Elbert wanted imprinted in his thoughts.

Chapter 10

After picking up Elbert from the bus terminal, Mrs. O'Malley drove the family Chevy station wagon back home. During the ride, Brendan peppered Elbert with questions. "You're so tall, can you dunk a basketball? Can you swim freestyle, two-lengths of the pool with the side-breathing method?"

Elbert relaxed after noticing that everyone seemed to be treating him normally. No one asked him if he was feeling "better." Instead it seemed as though everyone talked about what was going on in their lives. Little did he realize that Mrs. O'Malley had made it very clear to Jack and Brendan beforehand that they were not to treat Elbert any differently than they had prior to his father's death. "Even if he is quiet or reserved, don't ask him what's bothering him," she had counseled.

As the car neared the O'Malley's home, Elbert breathed in the view. Such an impressive contrast to his town. Rows and rows of townhomes and condominiums, high-rise office buildings, hotels and expansive shopping malls. And so many automobiles. The traffic at 5:30 pm was incredibly slow, even when Aunt Kathleen took a shortcut.

After arriving at the house, Elbert phoned his mother to let her know he'd arrived safely and partially unpacked his suitcase, using a dresser that Jack had cleared for him in his room. Walking out towards the living room, he heard Mrs. O'Malley holler from the kitchen.

"You boys can go outside and play. Elbert, I'm making a salad and spaghetti and meatballs in honor of your arrival, but it probably won't be ready for at least an hour. So go have fun for a little and leave me to my cooking – just be back inside in an hour."

The boys walked over to Dana's house and peered inside through the screen door at the Allens eating dinner in the dining room.

"Come on in, Jack," Mr. Allen shouted from the end of the table.

Jack introduced Elbert to the Allens, and Mrs. Allen asked if the boys would like to join them for supper.

"No thank you, Mrs. Allen," said Jack. "My mom is making dinner, but it won't be ready for about an hour."

Dana placed an ear of corn on the cob on her plate. "You two should go back into the woods," she suggested. "I saw Gary and Kenny head back there a few minutes before dinner. Just be sure to warn Elbert that Gary will probably refuse to allow you into his fort unless you kiss his butt."

"Watch your language, young lady," demanded Mrs. Allen, as Mr. Allen snickered quietly and shook his head. Jack even noticed that Elbert had a toothy grin on his face for the first time since arriving.

The boys said goodbye and walked back behind the Saunders' yard and down into the woods. When they arrived at the fort, Jack yelled, "Hey guys, my cousin Elbert is visiting from West Virginia."

Jack noticed that Gary had done a nice job of finishing up the fort. He had fastened a green plastic picnic tablecloth above the plywood roof to protect the wood from rain and applied a coat of green paint to the exterior to help the fort blend into the leaves of the tall oak. He also noticed that Gary had removed the temporary ladder, meaning that he must have installed a rope ladder and pulled it up into the fort.

"The fort looks great, Gary," said Jack. "Throw the rope ladder down so I can show Elbert what it looks like inside."

"You should have thought about that before you quit working with me on building the fort," said Gary. "Now only Kenny and I get to use it, so I hope you learned your lesson."

Elbert looked up into the tree and surmised that he could easily climb the tree without any kind of ladder, but instead nudged Jack and said, "It's okay, let's do a little exploring."

"Sorry about not letting you come into the fort, guys," Kenny yelled as the boys walked off. "I told Gary he should let you in. He made me give him my Carl Yastrzemski baseball card to let me in and when I told him I changed my mind and wanted it back, he said *no way*."

Jack and Elbert just headed further into the woods.

"I see that Gary hasn't changed since the last time I visited," Elbert observed.

The boys walked about sixty yards deeper into the forest and approached a creek that meandered through the full length of the wooded area. The creek was shallow, less than a foot deep in most areas and ranging in width from two to ten feet, depending on the amount of rain that had collected.

"Look at the moss growing on these rocks," Jack observed as he looked at a large pile of heavy stones on the side of the creek.

Lifting one to show his cousin, Jack failed to see the snake below that he'd inadvertently disturbed, but Elbert reacted as soon as he saw it. The snake made an aggressive move toward Jack, narrowly failing in its attempt to strike him, mainly because Jack had slipped backwards on the creek's bank and fallen on his rear. Grabbing a long tree limb from the ground nearby, Elbert used its jagged tip to pin the snake to the ground. The copperhead was angry, three feet of its tail shaking repeatedly and trying to escape from the pressure of the branch, while its head tried desperately to find a victim to sink its fangs into.

While applying pressure to the branch to keep the snake pinned, Elbert reached to his ankle with his right hand and removed a six-inch knife that was strapped to his leg. With one swift swing of the blade he severed the snake in two. Elbert then quickly slammed the tree branch down on the head of the snake with all of his might, crushing it on the bank of the creek.

Jack's eyes were as large as saucers, and his breath quickly caught up to his pounding heart. "You saved me, Elbert. I was frozen when I saw that snake jump at me. If I hadn't slipped backwards, he would have bit me. But you reacted so fast . . . And since when have you carried a knife on your leg?"

"You never know when a knife will come in handy – so when you need one, it probably isn't a good time to wish you had one," Elbert answered as he rinsed the blade in the creek and strapped it back to his calf. "You know, even after cutting that copperhead's body, its head could have still probably bitten you. A cold-blooded snake takes a while to die."

The boys walked another fifty yards into the woods, Jack now cautious to avoid stepping anywhere where he couldn't find snake-clear footing. They came upon an area that Jack had never explored. He'd always stayed inside the hundred-yard limit within which his parents had warned him to stay, but with Elbert, he always felt safe in pushing the limits.

About twenty yards further, through the trees and berry bushes, the boys noticed a grey wooden house. A gravel driveway wrapped around it, and led to a large adjacent barn. A light shined from the interior of the house and a porch lantern flickered dimly from the exterior. An old red pickup truck was parked in the driveway.

"I had no idea that there were any houses back in these woods," said Jack as he and Elbert stopped to listen for any sounds of movement. "I guess the driveway must connect to Annandale Road because it certainly doesn't have an entrance through our neighborhood."

Elbert examined the two structures. The house looked more like it belonged in West Virginia than a suburb of Washington DC. "Let's keep walking, maybe we will find even more houses back in this area."

Before they had completed another step, Jack and Elbert froze as a tall man, dressed in a black button-down shirt, black pants, and boots, stepped from behind a bush to their right. He held a 38-caliber revolver with a silver barrel and black handle. It looked similar to the gun Jack's father carried. The man pointed the barrel at the ground just in front of Elbert and Jack. His long black hair, unshaven face, and long sideburns went unnoticed to Jack, who was having difficulty looking beyond the barrel of the weapon.

In a deep, gruff voice, the man in black snarled, "You boys are trespassing. I don't ever want to see you snooping around here again. You hear?"

Without answering Elbert and Jack sprinted away, running as fast as they could, crossing over the creek, past the tree fort and out of the woods. Reaching Jack's front yard, the boys fell to the ground, lying on their backs as they tried to slow their racing hearts and catch their breath.

"That guy scared the crap out of me," said Jack as his breathing began to return to normal.

"I know what you mean," said Elbert. "He definitely didn't want anyone snooping around his home, and that gun of his definitely got my attention."

"Well that's one place I definitely will want to avoid in the future," said Jack.

"Are you kidding me, Jack? A guy like that, who would use a gun to scare a couple of kids . . . he must be up to something bad, and I'd like to figure out exactly what it is."

Chapter 11

Jimmy Szymanski entered the house, allowing the screen door to slam loudly against its frame. He needed a drink, and grabbed his last bottle of bourbon. Lifting it to the kitchen light, he cursed as he realized it was nearly empty. Drinking its last few drops, he tossed the bottle into the trash and looked at the clock on the wall above the kitchen table.

It was nearly 8:00 p.m. and George should have been here more than thirty minutes ago. Jimmy felt like a prisoner at the house in the woods, without a car. Despite Anthony Mancini's promises to install a new engine in his old pickup truck in the driveway, it remained unrepaired out on the gravel, rusting away from neglect and the weather.

"Finally!" he said to himself as he heard the sound of George's 66 Ford Falcon roll up and park behind the old pickup. Jimmy walked out the front door.

"It's about time you got here. Where the hell have you been?"

George DiCandilo got out of the car, and with his thick Brooklyn accent replied, "And it's nice to see you, too, Jimmy."

Opening the trunk of the Falcon, George removed two grocery bags, one with food for the kitchen and the other with four bottles of Jim Beam and a carton of Chesterfield cigarettes. Jimmy held the screen door open as George entered the house to set the bags on the kitchen counter. He immediately removed one of the fifths of bourbon from the bag, twisted the cap, and took a generous swig.

"So why are you in such a rosy mood this evening?" asked George as he emptied the groceries into the refrigerator and the cabinets.

"You'd be in a crappy mood too if you were stuck out here without a car, with no damn liquor or food except for a lousy loaf of bread," replied Jimmy, taking a second chug from the bottle.

In hopes of getting Jimmy out of his lousy frame of mind, George said, "Well, I picked up a couple of steaks to throw on the grill for dinner and then we can get to work. Tony wants us to run off fifteen grand in tens and twenties tonight." He paused, shaking his head in disgust. "And why don't you behave like a civilized human being and pour your bourbon into a glass?"

George poured three fingers into a tumbler he'd removed from the cabinet and, holding it out to Jimmy, exclaimed "Cheers" without expecting or receiving a response.

With the bourbon entering his bloodstream, Jimmy could now begin to feel the edges of his moodiness wearing off, as the warmth of the bourbon was hitting its mark and dulling his senses. It seemed ironic that what cost him and George their jobs at Anthony Mancini's printing company was their infatuation with Jim Beam, as heavy drinking seemed to them to be, more or less a part of the job description in that field. But their frequent week-long benders diminished the value they provided to the boss, in spite of their expertise as printers. Only now that Mancini's business had hit a rough patch did he have no choice but to offer them an "independent contractor project," as he called it. It allowed them to earn $500 in cash per week, along with food, booze, and a house to live in, out in the middle of the woods. Jimmy now realized that he should have negotiated for a car to be included in the deal, but then again, Tony had promised to get an engine for the truck.

Jimmy and George both realized that what they were doing was wrong. Printing counterfeit currency and circulating it into the economy was a federal offense, punishable by up to twenty years in prison. At age fifty-four, and with a liver that was already sending signals that it was wearing out, Jimmy realized that if they were ever arrested and convicted, it would likely be a life sentence for him. And at age fifty-eight, for George, it would undoubtedly be the same.

They were both certain that if they continued doing this work long enough, they would eventually be caught. So their goal was to save up $25,000 in cash each and then move to the coast of Mexico. In six months, they had saved up about $10,000 apiece, and with a little luck, they might be able to hit their goal by the end of the year. Especially if they implemented their plan to cut out Tony on their final payday. And if they ended up getting caught? Well, maybe that was the only way either Jimmy or George was ever going to stay off the booze for good.

George poured the charcoal into the grill kettle and squirted a stream of lighter fluid before throwing a match on the coals. He then cleaned the grate and wiped it with a paper towel that he'd dipped in vegetable oil. Once the coals had all heated, he placed the grate on the grill and threw on two large rib eyes. He poured a can of baked beans into a small pot, set it next to the steaks, and stirred them with a wooden spoon.

"I passed all of the bills today," said George. "I had to go down to 14th Street in DC, and you know how much I hate that place. But good old Fast Eddie came through with the ten G's." Stirring the beans, he paused before adding, "But I swear, that son-of-a-bitch is the scariest piece of shit I've ever met."

Jimmy took a sip from his bottle. "I've told you to pack a gun whenever you go to 14th street, but you never listen."

"Hell, I'd probably shoot myself. And Fast Eddie knows how to use a gun a lot better than me," said George as he checked the steaks. "Afterwards, I met with Tony at the drive-in parking lot and he gave us $500 each in cash and $100 for food and booze… and he told me to tell you that he is having a guy stop out on Sunday or Monday to pick up the truck and put an engine in. It should be back within a couple of days."

It upset Jimmy to think of their deal with Tony. First of all, the bastard had fired them from his printing business, and now they were doing all of the work and he was keeping close to ninety percent of the cash from their printing and circulation duties. Whenever George visited with Fast Eddie or with any of the other drug dealers or pimps who they passed the counterfeit cash to, they were paid thirty to thirty-five cents on the dollar for their trouble. But dealing with these types of lowlifes carried the risk that on any given day they could simply take the cash and put a bullet in our skull. All while Tony sat in his big mansion, with his fancy cars, never risking his fat ass with any of the dirty work.

Although he felt resentment, Jimmy also realized that he and George needed Tony. He owned the expensive printing press, the plates, the cameras, and cutting machine that resided in the barn's office. And Tony was the person who provided them with the expensive Crane currency paper. The paper was made up of linen and fiber that created a strong but flexible bond, which to the touch felt just like the real thing.

George and Jimmy had the skill to run the press and to print and cut the notes, but without Tony's equipment they would not have what was needed to get the job done. But ninety percent for Tony? It just didn't sit well with Jimmy. But he was certain this would all change on their last score, before they split for Mexico.

As they devoured their steak and bean dinner, Jimmy brought up scaring the crap out of two kids who were snooping around in the woods near the house. "You should have seen the little kid, I thought he was going to piss his pants. The taller kid gave me a strange look, but once they saw my gun and I told them they were trespassing they ran so fast that I don't think we'll ever see them again."

"You stupid Polack!" shouted George. "Why in God's name are you walking in the woods, carrying your gun? Those kids could have run home and told their parents, and the next thing you know the police will be breathing up our asses to check us out. We need to lay low here, and if some kid happens to be out exploring in the woods, we need to be friendly. Don't send them any signals. Do you get what I mean?"

"I was just walking around having a smoke," explained Jimmy, "and I saw the kids come across a Copperhead. So, I pulled out my gun in case the snake got the better of them, but that tall kid . . . he knew how to handle himself. Chopped the damn thing in two . . . crushed its head with a branch. I wasn't trying to scare them with the gun, but it was fun to watch the little bastards sprint for home."

After finishing their meals, George picked up the plates and headed to the house to rinse them in the sink. "Just don't scare any kids anymore. If they come back around again, tell them that you didn't mean to scare them, and keep the damn gun hidden away. I'm going to clean up the kitchen, then I'll join you in the office. Let's set up the first batch of twenties for printing."

Chapter 12

After dinner, Mrs. O'Malley asked Jack and Elbert if they wanted to go out and play for another hour or so. Brendan wanted to protest that he wasn't being included but knew that his mother would tell him it was time for his bath because he had swim practice in the morning.

"I need to get in my run and a quick workout that should only take about twenty minutes and then we can hang out in the cul-de-sac with Dana and whoever else is around. Do you want to join me in the run?" asked Jack of his cousin.

"No thanks, Jack. I need to finish unpacking a few things and then I'll wait outside for you until you are finished," replied Elbert.

Jack stretched his calf muscles, and Elbert waited until his cousin had headed out the door before going to Jack's room, removing a couple of items from his suitcase, and heading outside. Noticing Gary, Brian, and Dana sitting in Dana's yard, he quickly ran across the street, cutting through the Atkins yard, where he could hear a radio broadcast of a baseball game playing from a portable radio near the house, but no one was sitting in either of the lawn chairs next to the radio's table.

Elbert glanced at the shed in the back of the yard, where the door was open and a light was on. Hearing someone rummaging inside, he ran quietly behind the shed and then sprinted along the back edge of the yard, crossing through to the Allen's and then to the Saunders' backyard before slipping down the hill into the woods.

He removed a small flashlight from his pocket and turned it on, pointing it down towards the ground. The moonlight enabled him to have a good view of the trees above, but it did little to help Elbert know where to dodge brush or to find firm footing. He made his way quickly to the tree fort. Gary had left the rope ladder down when he left, so Elbert quickly climbed the rope and entered the fort. He peered out of the rear opening that Gary had built to serve as a window – and which faced towards the house and barn that he and Jack had stumbled upon after killing the snake. He could just make out a couple of lights through the trees; pulling out a small pair of binoculars, he held them up to the lights, but branches and leaves from the oak tree blocked his view.

He leaned out of the fort and climbed to a higher branch, pulling out his knife and cutting off the leaves and branches that were within reach. As the foliage fell to the ground, he now had a view of the barn. With his binoculars he could now clearly see the front door to the barn, as well as a small bench that rested outside the door to the right, just underneath a dimly lit lamp illuminating the gravel driveway.

He watched as, after a moment, the tall thin man dressed in black came out of the barn. The man sat on the bench, lifted what looked like a bottle of liquor, and took a sip. A moment later, another man, slightly shorter and of more muscular build, approached the barn carrying a box. He took it into the barn's office and a few seconds later joined the man in black on the bench. The man in black poured some of his alcohol in a glass for the second man. Then they both drank and stood, rather slowly, heading back into the barn in a woozy fashion.

Elbert climbed back down the tree rope and ran from the woods. When he reached Jack's front yard, he sat in the grass to mentally review what he had learned. The fort could be used as a spot to keep an eye on what was going on outside of the barn, but it did not provide any view of the house. And two grown men, both of whom seemed to enjoy getting drunk, were apparently working on something at night in the barn. Maybe they were just organizing their barn, and liked to drink while they did it. But why would one of them go walking around their property carrying a pistol, and why did he feel that he needed to scare a couple of kids who were just out for a walk in the woods? One thing was for sure: Elbert knew what he was going to be doing later tonight while everyone else was sleeping in the O'Malley house.

Chapter 13

Elbert waited for an hour after Aunt Kathleen had gone to bed before quietly slipping out of the house. He told himself that it was a good thing that Uncle Jack was out of town on an assignment, because he recalled that he was a light sleeper and surely would have heard Elbert moving about.

The night air felt warm but without the humidity that lingered earlier in the evening. The moon cascaded a dim light on the cul-de-sac, illuminated more brightly by the street lamp in front of the Tuckers' house. Elbert strapped his knife to his ankle and placed the binoculars and flashlight in his pockets and jogged into the woods behind the Saunders' home.

As he approached the tree fort he quickly ascended the rope ladder and removed the binoculars. The lights he saw earlier coming from the house and the barn were no longer visible, confirming that the men he had seen earlier had either left or gone to sleep. Without light from the barn, it took him a few moments to locate the building through his binoculars, but finally he spotted it and could make out its gray walls and white door.

Elbert's plan was to covertly approach the barn and see if he could enter the building or at least look inside through the window in the door. If spotted by either of the two men he had seen, he felt as though he could outrun them, especially knowing that they were probably both still feeling the effects of the booze they'd been consuming.

He climbed out of the fort and began moving towards the house. With his flashlight shining on the ground in front of him, he used his free hand to shade the light from glowing outwardly to avoid him being spotted from the house or barn. When he approached the creek, he glanced at the dead snake that he'd killed before leaping across. As he neared the men's property, he ducked behind a tall row of ferns growing just beyond the driveway.

Twenty yards to his left stood the barn, twenty yards directly in front of him the house, where he presumed the men were sleeping. Both single-story buildings were constructed of wood, and neither looked as though it had seen a fresh drop of paint in years. Blotches of black dirt or mold appeared on the walls and the roof of the house and it appeared to be missing a few shingles. In the driveway, he saw the old red pickup truck and a white Ford Falcon that he did not recall seeing earlier. A picnic table stood to the left of the house along with a grill and a couple of metal trashcans overflowing with garbage.

Elbert slowly walked towards the edge of the barn, trying to step lightly on the pebble driveway. When approaching the small wooden porch out front, he paused as a raccoon scurried in front of him, hissing and growling as it made its way toward the house.

He approached the barn's office door and tried the knob, but it had been locked. He looked through the window on the door, but with the reflection from the moonlight found it difficult to see much inside.

He was able to make out what appeared to be a large bench, with a large machine or piece of equipment on top, but without adequate lighting he simply couldn't identify what type of machine it was. He saw a box, probably the one the man had carried into the barn earlier, and could make out the name Crane in dark letters on the side of the box. With nothing left to see through the front window, he decided to walk around the barn to determine if there were any other entrances or windows, but found only two large wooden barn doors to the right that both were locked.

Elbert next moved to the truck and the car in the driveway, looking through the windows to see what he might find. Finding the car keys still in the trunk lock of the Ford Falcon, he quietly turned the key and looked inside using his flashlight. Dozens of packs of cigarettes and chewing gum littered the space in front of the car's spare tire.

As he closed the trunk quietly, making sure he heard the click of the lock, a loud noise rang near the house. Elbert retreated behind the ferns and lay on the ground, but discovered the racket had just been a trashcan that had been overturned by the raccoon as it scavenged for food. After seeing no disturbance from the men inside of the house, he decided to call off his search for the evening.

Maybe I am wasting my time, he thought disappointedly as he exited the woods. As he jogged back to the O'Malley's, Elbert realized that if he wanted to know what was going on at the house he was either going to have to catch the men while they were in the barn or break into the barn while they were asleep. By the time he'd laid his head back on his pillow in Jack's room, he'd already figured out which choice he would pursue. But to do so would require his cousin's assistance.

Chapter 14

On Saturday morning, Jack woke at about 7:00 am and noticed Elbert was still sound asleep. He quietly got dressed, went to the kitchen, and scrambled two eggs for breakfast. After preparing a piece of buttered toast, Jack went outside to bring in the morning edition of the *Washington Post*.

He focused his attention on a photo of Vice President Hubert Humphrey, who was giving a campaign speech in Michigan, to see if he could spot his father in the crowd in front of the podium, as he knew that he'd been traveling with the Vice President's protective detail on a series of campaign stops that week. His dad was expected home later today and would remain home for at least a few days before having to resume a busy period of protective work heading up to the national conventions.

The front-runners for each party appeared to be Humphrey for the Democrats, with Senator Eugene McCarthy still holding an outside shot, and Richard Nixon for the Republicans. Jack found himself favoring McCarthy. Not because McCarthy was adamantly opposed to the war in Vietnam, something Jack had not formed an opinion on, but because he seemed unafraid to oppose a sitting president. Jack liked how he made his case in public, unafraid of those who labeled him as a "dove" because of his call for an immediate withdrawal of U.S. troops from Vietnam. Jack always pulled for the underdog, and something about the personalities of both Nixon and Humphrey didn't spark his enthusiasm.

With Elbert still sleeping, Jack decided now would be a good time for him to get in his daily exercises and his run. He quietly grabbed his dumbbells from his room and went outside to complete his push-ups, sit-ups, and weight work, and then walked to the end of his street to begin his one-mile run. During the sprint interval, Jack noticed how his legs and lungs had become more conditioned to the faster pace and how it was easier for him to extend the sprint to 150 yards and reduce the jogging distance to 250 yards before the next sprint began.

After finishing his run, Jack returned to the house and was greeted by his mother, who was finishing her coffee while reading the paper. "Well Hello, Mr. Early-Bird," she said with a smile.

Jack liked how his Mom always seemed to be in a good mood each morning, but undoubtedly her spirit today was buoyed by the fact that Jack's dad would be returning from his trip. "Hi Mom, what time are you expecting Dad to get home?"

"He told me that he should be home by noon and to tell you that he would take you to baseball practice at two. Do you think that Elbert would want to come along and watch you practice?"

Jack hadn't mentioned anything about his practice to Elbert, so he really had no idea if he would want to sit around for a couple of hours to hear Coach Russell shouting instructions to him and his teammates. "Not sure. I haven't asked him yet, but since the concession stand is open on Saturdays . . . chances are he'll want to come - just to get a snow cone."

"Did I hear something about snow cones?" asked a groggy-looking Elbert, standing in pajamas that he seemed to have outgrown by six inches in his sleep. "What time is it?

"It's a little before nine. You just needed to catch up on your rest. Yesterday was a long day for you, with the bus trip and all. I'll bet you could use some breakfast?" suggested Mrs. O'Malley.

It had been an extremely long day for Elbert, especially considering his nocturnal pursuit in the woods. "Breakfast would be great. Do you have any Cheerios?" he asked.

"We always have Cheerios," responded Mrs. O'Malley. "Jack and Brendan couldn't live without them. Let me get you a bowl."

"Thanks, Aunt Kathleen," said Elbert, holding an envelope and a small package. "Last night, I forgot that my mom gave me a present to deliver, to thank you for letting me visit." The package was wrapped in bright red paper and tied with a white ribbon and a small pink bow. He handed it to his aunt along with the personal note from his mother. "Thanks, Aunt Kathleen, for allowing me to visit," he said as he handed the gift and card to her.

"It's our pleasure to have you here, Elbert. That sister of mine didn't need to bother with any gift for me. Having you visit is the only gift that we ever hoped for," she replied, as she opened the envelope and read the note written on her sister's personal stationery out loud so the boys could share in her message. *"To the best little sister I could ever ask for – even if you are my only little sister! Thank you for allowing Elbert to visit. I know he is looking forward to having a wonderful time with you and Jack and Jackie and Brendan. Please call me if you need anything. I thought you might like the little gift that I picked out for you.*

Love forever –Marcia"

Jack's mother untied the ribbon and removed the wrapping from the box. Lifting the lid, she held up two gold hoop earrings, each with a small aquamarine stone at its base.

She smiled. "I can't believe she remembered. When we were visiting West Virginia last year, I complimented your mom on her beautiful earrings . . . and now she decided to get me a pair just like them. I will have to send her a thank you note today. She is so thoughtful."

"Cool earrings, Mom . . . is it your birthday?" asked Brendan, who had entered the room and already grabbed a bowl and a spoon to join Elbert for breakfast.

"No. It's just a very thoughtful gift from your Aunt Marcia, thanking me for inviting Elbert."

"Elbert, did your mom give you a gift to give to me?" asked a hopeful Brendan.

"I'm afraid not, Brendan. But she did tell me to give you a hug and a kiss from her," said Elbert with arms wide, acting as though he wanted to give his little cousin a big hug and a kiss.

"Please," said Brendan. "Can't you see that I'm eating?"

Jack picked up the earrings. "Mom, these are really beautiful!"

Elbert's attention, on the other hand, had been drawn to the stationery card from his mother that was turned upside down on the table. At the bottom of the personalized note card was the name of the stationery manufacturer.

Crane . . .

Chapter 15

After arriving home from his trip, Jack's father unpacked his suitcase and changed into his weekend attire of broken-in khaki pants and a white button-down with navy stripes. Slipping on a pair of brown penny loafers without socks and rolling up the sleeves of his shirt, he walked into the living room and asked Jack and Elbert if they were ready to head out to the park.

Elbert was eager to attend baseball practice for two reasons. One, he was looking forward to having some time with his favorite uncle. Elbert always found Uncle Jack to be easy to talk to, and he couldn't remember having a conversation with an adult besides his mom in more than three months. Second, he had just heard that there were snow cones available at the park's concession stand.

As Mr. O'Malley turned left on Annandale Road, Elbert stared closely at the tree line to the left, looking for a driveway that could lead to the mysterious house in the woods. Then he noticed an unpaved, gravel road guarded by a small sign that read *"Private Property - No Trespassing"* and a dark, rusty chain that roped off the entrance. He looked for other driveways as they continued moving up the road, but no others appeared for more than half a mile. This had to be the driveway to the house in the woods, thought Elbert.

On the ride to the park, Jack's father told the boys that tonight he was planning on grilling up burgers and hot dogs, while Jack's mom would be whipping up her homemade baked beans with bacon, along with her cucumber salad and some fresh slices of watermelon. Jack peppered his father with questions about the Presidential election and whether he thought Senator McCarthy had any chance of winning the nomination from Vice President Humphrey.

"Honestly, I don't follow the polls, so I don't have any opinion on his chances," said Mr. O'Malley, "but from what I gather, it seems that Humphrey has the momentum and has a much better organization throughout the country. And since losing in the California primary and the death of Senator Kennedy, it doesn't appear that McCarthy is aggressively campaigning like he was previously."

When they arrived at the park, Jack ran off to join Coach Russell, who was headed towards field number three with his little red and white cooler in tow, while Randy and Adam Titus, the team's catcher, lugged the equipment bags up ahead.

"I see that your Dad was able to come out to watch practice today," said the coach, while spitting tobacco juice on the grass.

"Yes, sir. He just got back in town and he's going to be able to come to our game on Monday evening, plus I have my cousin Elbert, who is visiting from West Virginia, here as well. I told him about the snow cones!"

"How old is that cousin of yours?" asked Coach.

"He's thirteen. But he's big for his age," responded Jack.

Coach Russell shook his head. "I'd say so. He looks as big as some high-school seniors. I'd love to see someone with his size and strength batting cleanup for the Pirates."

"Well, who knows, Coach? If I can keep improving on hitting the curve, maybe one day you'll just have to put me at cleanup," said Jack with a grin, as he jogged ahead to join his teammates.

As the team went through its stretching and warmup session, Elbert and Uncle Jack walked over to the concession stand to pick up a couple of snow cones. Uncle Jack ordered his with cherry syrup, while Elbert chose the "Rainbow" option with cherry, grape, and lemon lime all combined into one cone. They walked back to the spectator stands where Jack's father greeted a few of the other parents that came to observe the team's final practice before their big game with the Cardinals. The parents all knew that if the Pirates could win this game, the Cardinals would be eliminated from the league title. But if they lost, they would likely be the Pirates' opponent in a playoff game for the championship.

Elbert and Uncle Jack took their seats near the top row of the bleachers and watched as the boys went through their wind sprints.

"Jack looks like a speed demon out there," remarked Elbert. "I don't know if his teammates are giving it their all, but Jack seems to be smoking everyone in those sprints."

"He's been working hard on his running and his strength, but he'd give anything to have a little of your height and weight. I've told him not to worry about it and that eventually he'll hit his growth spurt," said Mr. O'Malley.

"Well you know, Uncle Jack, sometimes kids in school don't cut their classmates any slack when it comes to your size," said Elbert, pausing to drink in a bit of the syrup from his snow cone. "So, it's probably more useful for you to tell the bullies at school that he'll eventually hit his growth spurt than it is for you to tell Jack."

"I know what you mean," said Mr. O'Malley. "But you know, learning how to deal with bullies and wise guys is one of the necessary lessons of growing up that everyone needs to experience. And nobody said that growing up in life was ever guaranteed to be easy and stress free."

During batting practice, Coach Russell threw to each of the players, and during Jack's turn at the plate he hit five fastballs solidly, with one ball clearing the left-field fence and two others blasted solidly into the left- and right-field gaps. Mr. O'Malley noticed how Jack seemed to tilt his head slightly downward before each pitch, a technique that he had been working on to concentrate on the release of the ball from the pitcher's hand. Though Jack swung early on one of the curves his coach threw, he hit two solid grounders and one long line drive on the three other curves that he was thrown. Mr. O'Malley could clearly see that his son's efforts at hitting the curve were paying off and that he was no longer bailing out of the batter's box as soon as he saw a pitch breaking towards the inside portion of the plate.

"Great job, Jack!" yelled Coach Russell. "Did you see the red circle on the ball as it left my hand?"

"Thanks, Coach. I didn't see the circle, but I really do think I'm starting to see the rotation of the seams," said Jack as he grabbed his glove and made his way back out to right field.

"Jack is really hitting the ball solidly," said Elbert. "That home run he hit was smacked so hard it could have cleared a fence that was thirty feet deeper."

"I think that's the first home run that I've ever seen him hit, even if it was only in a practice. We'll have to reward him with a snow cone when practice ends," said Mr. O'Malley.

"Maybe I should get a second one, as well. After all, we don't want to make him feel bad by eating his alone," Elbert replied to Mr. O'Malley's laughter. "Uncle Jack," he added tentatively, "I was thinking of getting my Mom some new stationery for her birthday. I know the brand that she likes. It's made by a company named Crane. You wouldn't have any idea where I could find Crane stationery in this area, would you?"

"It's funny that you mention Crane. They make some of the finest paper in the world, using cotton and linen fibers. In fact, they produce the paper used to make U.S. currency. As part of our training, we visited their plant in Maine to learn about how the paper is made and what differentiates our U.S. currency paper from other paper sold elsewhere."

"Why do Secret Service agents need to learn about this type of paper?" asked Elbert with genuine curiosity.

"We're a part of the Treasury Department," replied Mr. O'Malley, "and a big part of our work outside of protection is in law enforcement related to financial crimes like forgeries and counterfeiting. I spent eight years of my career working in the counterfeit division. We pick up a couple of million dollars of counterfeits each year."

"Do counterfeiters use the same paper that the Treasury Department uses when they make their phony money?" asked Elbert.

"They'd like to. But Crane has an exclusive agreement with our government. No one can purchase the same paper that is used for our currency. But they make other currency paper that is very similar in quality. So that's how I've learned quite a bit about Crane," said Mr. O'Malley.

"Do you have any idea where I might be able to get some of their stationery cards for my Mom?" asked Elbert.

"Not really. But my guess is wherever fine cards and stationery are sold. You might need to check the Yellow Pages. But their products are pricey, so you might want to check out some other brands," explained Mr. O'Malley.

Chapter 16

After arriving home, Mr. O'Malley suggested that the boys go play for an hour or so while he prepared the grill for dinner. Jack dropped off his baseball gear and joined Elbert on the front terrace.

"I hope it wasn't too boring for you to have to sit through my practice?" asked Jack.

"Actually, it was perfect," said Elbert, deciding that now was the time to bring Jack up to speed on what he had been learning. "First of all, I enjoyed not one, but two rainbow snow cones, and secondly I had a chance to watch you smack a line drive over the left-field fence. I noticed how you really extended your arms, without over swinging. You really connected solidly. Your swing seems compact, too. Not a lot of wasted effort."

Jack was always amazed at Elbert's ability to pay attention to details that most people overlooked. "Thanks for the feedback. Coach Russell has really worked with me on my stance and my swing and has spent a lot of time on keeping my head leaning in. I used to have a tendency to pull my head away from the pitch, especially on curves, or anything that seemed to be thrown inside. Plus he deliberately throws his practice pitches at faster speeds than we see in games to help us feel comfortable and make the best contact."

"I also enjoyed getting a chance to talk to your dad," continued Elbert. "I've always been comfortable talking with him . . . I guess because he never seems to be judging me and he always seems to remember what it was like to be a kid. You know my dad always considered your father to be someone he admired and was proud to have not only as a brother-in-law but also as a friend. And Dad never liked phonies, or people who acted like they were better than others. So I know he thought your dad was smart, fun to be with, and genuine. Plus, he said your dad could read people almost immediately and know how to adjust in dealing with them intuitively. Maybe it's from his training with the Secret Service."

The conversation about his father caused Elbert to pause as his eyes watered.

"Every time I think of my dad I keep wondering," he said as he put a hand to his face to hide his tears, "if I'm ever going to be able to not feel like I have a giant hole inside of me, without him." His words were cut off as he choked to catch his breath.

Jack looked at his cousin in a way that, without words, communicated that he understood. Finally, he developed the courage to say, "I know that if it were me, I'd feel exactly the same. The only thing I know for sure is that your dad was so proud of you." Jack's eyes teared up along with his cousin's, reminding him that although his hole might have been smaller, he too felt the loss of Uncle Bert.

Elbert pulled the front of his shirt over his face to wipe his eyes and nose. "I went back to that house in the woods last night. In fact, I went back twice."

Jack had suspected that this subject would re-emerge. Elbert craved adventure and was the most curious person he'd encountered. At the same time, he was intuitive, and must have understood that the man they had encountered had scared Jack and that he would never want to see him, or his gun, again.

Elbert filled him in on the details. He told him how, with binoculars, you could see the barn, even at night, from the tree fort.

He told him about the second man he'd spotted and their obvious appetite for alcohol, mentioning the light in the office of the barn as well as what he had seen through the office window and what he had found in the Ford Falcon's trunk.

"So, what you are saying," said Jack, hoping to convince his cousin to lessen his curiosity, "is that all you've discovered is that two guys have an office in a barn, where for all you know they store their whiskey. And that the guy with the Ford likes to smoke cigarettes and chew gum. I'll bet if you walked into all of the homes in the woods of West Virginia, you'd find liquor, cigarettes, and guns in most of them, and most of their owners would threaten anyone who trespassed on their property. Don't you think you're making more out of this than it deserves?"

"You're probably right," replied Elbert, "but until I learn more about what's inside that barn, I won't know for sure. And there's one other thing that I did spot in the barn's office."

Elbert explained the box he could see with the name Crane printed on its side. He then mentioned how he again saw Crane on the stationery card his mother had sent with the gift he'd given to Aunt Kathleen. And finally, he told him about his conversation with Jack's dad about Crane being noted for its currency paper.

"Are you trying to say that the guy we saw in the woods is a counterfeiter? How do you know that they don't have a typewriter in the barn's office and the Crane paper is simply used for typing on the same stationery that your mom uses because they send out a lot of thank-you notes? Heck, Elbert, they could have a Crane box that they use to store their whiskey. And did you ever think that there might be more than one company named Crane?" asked Jack.

"Jack, I'm not trying to say that I have reached any conclusions. You might be right that I'm just letting my curiosity get the best of me. But tell me this. Did the guy we saw in the woods with the gun look like the kind of guy who sends out a lot of thank-you notes, or for that matter, like the type of guy who would use the finest, most expensive stationery to do his typing on?"

He paused, seeing hesitation in Jack's eyes, and after emphasizing that he would need Jack's help to learn enough to determine if he was right and they should just let it go, Jack relented. Soon the two boys were back in the woods, climbing into the tree fort and looking out at the barn through binoculars. Jack could see the two men entering and exiting the office and occasionally sitting on the bench out front to drink from a bottle of whiskey.

"I'm not going to be able to get you to drop this, am I?" asked Jack.

With a broad smile on his face, Elbert tousled his cousin's hair. "I knew you'd come around sooner or later. Once I tell you my plans, I know you'll feel a lot more comfortable. But for now let's get back to your house. I think I can smell my burger on the grill!"

As they walked back to the O'Malley house, Elbert felt slightly ashamed that he had overstated how comfortable Jack would feel once he knew the plan he had concocted. If Jack only knew that he still hadn't been able to come up with a plan, perhaps he wouldn't have agreed to help.

As the boys passed through the Saunders' yard, Elbert spotted Brendan and Bruce trying to hide behind the Swansons' hedgerow.

"What's up guys?" asked Elbert, as he and Jack walked towards the two boys trying, unsuccessfully, to hide on the ground, their faces down, arms covering their heads.

"You know, Brendan, just because you can't see us, doesn't mean that we can't see you," said Jack to his younger brother.

Peeking out above his arms, Brendan showed a worried expression. Putting his head back down to avoid facing his brother and cousin, he asked, "Do you promise to keep a secret if I tell you what we have done, and will you promise to help us?"

Realizing that Brendan would never tell him anything unless he complied, Jack agreed, and Brendon sat up on the lawn with Bruce following suit.

"Well," Brendan began nervously, "Bruce and I wanted to use your pellet gun. So I snuck into the attic and found it where Mom thought she'd hid it, in the old cabinet where she keeps some of our old winter coats. She kept the box of pellets hidden in the pocket of her long black coat with the furry collar. So anyway, we got the gun and the pellets while you two and Dad were at practice and we started shooting over the hedge at leaves in the trees. But that got a little bit boring, so we saw a bird land on a branch and I took a shot at it, and I swear I didn't think I would hit it. I just figured I would scare it."

"But he hit it right in the neck and it fell to the ground like a rock," said Bruce. "And then this other bird, it must have been its mother or its baby . . . it starts screeching. I swear it sounded like it was crying. Look over in the yard, it's still screeching."

The boys stared at the dead dove on the ground behind the rock garden in the O'Malleys' backyard. The other dove was flying nearby, frantically crying out. Jack looked towards the house where smoke from the barbeque floated into the air.

"Burgers should be ready in five or ten minutes," they heard Jack's father call to his mother in the house. "Have the kids come back yet?"

Elbert realized that if Mr. O'Malley walked back to the rock garden, he would find the dead bird. If he saw it, would he be able to tell that it had been shot? Glancing into the Swansons' yard, Elbert saw their dark gray cat, Smokey, crouched near the hedgerow, peering towards the screeching dove.

"Where's the pellet gun and the pellets?" he assertively asked Brendan.

Brendan pointed to a bush about fifteen feet away.

"Jack, you grab the gun and pellets."

While Jack went to retrieve the items, Elbert picked up Smokey and quickly lowered him over the hedgerow, near the dead bird. Once he saw the cat head in the direction of the bird, Elbert ran to Jack and grabbed the gun and pellets.

"Ok. I'll take these to a safe place," said Elbert, now in action mode. "Jack, you take Brendan into your house and get cleaned up for dinner. Tell your mom that I was collecting some honeysuckle in the woods and will be just a couple of minutes behind. Bruce, are you joining us for dinner or are you eating at your house?"

Elbert quickly directed everyone to their places and hustled into the woods with the pellet gun and pellets in tow. Since Bruce was invited to have dinner with the O'Malleys, he went with Jack and Brendan to their house, and all three boys went into the bathroom to wash their hands.

Elbert reached the tree fort and climbed the rope swing with the pellet gun in hand and the box of pellets tucked into his pants. He then carefully slid the pellet rifle underneath the plastic picnic tablecloth that protected the roof of the fort. There it would be unlikely that Gary or any of the other kids who came to the fort would discover what he had hidden. As he left the fort and sprinted back to the O'Malleys' for dinner, a look of satisfaction crept over his face, knowing that a part of his plan was beginning to come together.

After saying the blessing, Brendan looked nervously at Bruce as Smokey came across the yard with the dead dove firmly in its mouth.

"Looks like we figured out what that bird was screeching at a few minutes ago," said Mr. O'Malley to his wife. "Bruce, it looks like Smokey is back to his hunting again."

Brendan looked at his Mom, blurting, "Mom, these are the best baked beans you've ever made, and Dad, this cheeseburger is perfect. Can I have another piece of watermelon, please?"

Mrs. O'Malley smiled as she passed the watermelon, happy to see that her youngest son's appetite had miraculously improved in just a matter of seconds.

After dinner, Mrs. O'Malley cleaned the dishes and straightened up the kitchen, while her husband made a large pitcher of Manhattans – their favorite adult drink –combining bourbon, vermouth, bitters, and Brendan's favorite, maraschino cherries. He carried the concoction out to the patio, where Mr. and Mrs. Allen, Dana's parents, would soon join them, with candles lit for the occasion. There, they would remain for a couple of hours, telling stories and enjoying quite a few laughs, along with a second or third pour into their Manhattan glasses.

Jack loved Saturday evenings during the summer in his neighborhood. He enjoyed listening to the sounds of his parents' laughter with the Allens as they traded jokes and stories while listening to the mellow, baritone sound of Frank Sinatra albums. He enjoyed the sound of the Senators baseball games playing from Mr. Atkins' radio, the warm weather, and lying barefoot in the grass in his blue jeans and tee shirt. He loved the smells of the summer evening. A freshly mowed lawn, the scent of juniper and pine, and the clean smell of Dana's recently shampooed hair whenever they played together, catching fireflies in a glass pickle jar or inspecting beetles in the dirt. Tonight, Jack walked Elbert to the back of the Atkins' house to re-introduce his cousin to Mr. Atkins.

"Hi Mr. . . . hmmm . . . I mean, Nelly," Jack recovered before Mr. Atkins could correct him. "How are the Senators doing tonight?"

"Ha, Jack my boy," said Nelly. "Good to see you again, and it's especially nice to see you again, Elbert. I think it's probably been two years since I saw you and I swear it looks like you have grown a foot since then. I mean . . . ha, son, you look like you're ready to join the Army!"

"It's nice to see you again too, Mr. Atkins. I've grown quite a bit over the last two years, but since I'm only thirteen, I don't think the Army would be too interested in me, at least for a few more years."

"Ha!" bellowed Mr. Atkins. "Being too young didn't stop me from joining the Army, and hell, son, you're a lot bigger and stronger than I was when I snuck in at age seventeen. And please, call me Nelly. None of that Mr. Atkins nonsense. Ha! Now Jack, I purposely loaded up the freezer in the shed with popsicles, so you and your cousin can join me whenever you want to listen to some baseball." Pausing, he added, "Why don't you go grab a couple of them? And ha, while you're at it, pour me one of those Ballantines in my coffee mug."

Jack grabbed the mug and headed back into the shed to retrieve a bottle of beer from the refrigerator. Snapping off the lid, he tilted the mug sideways as he poured to prevent it from foaming up, like he'd seen his dad do when he poured a beer. Afterwards he placed the empty bottle into the crate of bottles that Mr. Atkins kept on a shelf next to the refrigerator, and grabbed one grape- and one cherry-flavored popsicle from the freezer before turning off the light on his way out of the shed.

"Thank you, Jack," said Mr. Atkins as he took the mug from Jack. "Cheers," he said, then shouted "Plasma!" as an expression of appreciation after having tasted the cold beer.

"Surprise me," said Elbert to Jack when he asked him which flavor he preferred.

Jack kept the cherry popsicle and gave the other to his cousin. The boys sat and smiled as Nelly complained about the way the Senators were playing that evening, trailing the Baltimore Orioles three-two in the bottom of the sixth inning.

"Pascual has pitched solidly and Hondo hit one of his monster home runs, but McMullen made a throwing error trying to start a double play, leading to two unearned runs for the O's," said Nelly as he lit up a cigarette. "We're already twenty games behind in the standings and if we lose tonight the Senators will be fifteen games under .500 for the season. I need to get my head examined to figure out why I follow this team, game-in and game-out."

"I always figured you just loved to sit outside even if there wasn't a baseball game, enjoying a smoke and of course a mug full of your *special coffee*. For you, the ball game is just a bonus," said Jack as he winked at Nelly.

"Ha, You're right about that, Jack. Even when there's a rainout I still come out and just sit in the chair in the shed and putter around for a couple of hours while listening to music. In fact, I was in the shed a couple of times this week and watched you boys running back and forth from the woods. Do you boys have a tree house or something back there?"

"Actually, it's Gary's tree fort," Jack said uneasily. "But we've gone into it a couple of times when Gary wasn't around. You know, yesterday, Elbert killed a copperhead snake that I accidentally disturbed?"

Jack was pleased with himself for how he had changed the subject so smoothly.

"How big was it?" Mr. Atkins quizzed Elbert. "Was it aggressive? How did you react so quickly? How did you kill it?"

In between bites of his popsicle, Elbert calmly described how he used a stick to pin the snake to the ground and his knife to sever it a few inches from the head. "It's not the first time I'd encountered a copperhead. My Dad taught me how to use a stick or a pole or any type of long object to keep it at a distance until it can be contained. We also found a house with a barn, back in the woods. Did you know there was a house back in the woods, Nelly?"

"Can't say that I did," responded Nelly, "but then again I rarely have wandered off very far in those woods. I imagine it must be off Annandale Road."

"Yes sir, it is." said Elbert. "It's interesting, after we encountered the snake, a man who lives at that house told us we were trespassing, and he was carrying a gun."

Nelly took another swig from his mug and set it down on the table. "Was the property posted with private property notices, or trespassing signs?"

"No sir, at least none that we saw," said Jack.

"Well, if someone owns property that borders public land, they need to have it posted or at least have it fenced off if they expect to keep it private," said Nelly. "But if I were you boys, I'd stay away from it anyway, just to be safe. What type of gun was he carrying, a rifle or a handgun?"

"It was a handgun, like a police revolver, maybe a .38. It wasn't the type of gun you typically see someone carry who might be hunting for an animal. At least that's how it seemed to me," said Elbert.

"Well like I said, you boys should be careful back there just to stay on the safe side," warned Nelly. "Ha Jack . . . do you think you can get me a refill on this coffee? Ha?" He laughed loudly as Jack grabbed the mug and jogged back to the shed.

"I've never been a big fan of guns," Nelly said to Elbert. "They should only be used in war and for hunting." He paused. "During my time in the Army, I guess I saw more than my share of what people with guns are capable of doing."

Elbert looked at Nelly and calmly replied, "My dad taught me how to shoot a rifle. We'd hunt deer, but honestly, I just enjoyed testing my accuracy with the Remington bolt-action rifle. I've never been a fan of venison, probably because it tastes a little gamey, and my dad always said, *'If* we *won't eat it, we won't hunt it.'* So I never actually shot a deer myself. But I did enjoy target shooting, and my dad definitely taught me how to do that well."

After Jack returned with the mug of beer for Mr. Atkins, the boys said goodbye and went back to the O'Malleys' house. They decided that they wouldn't go back into the woods until Tuesday, when Jack's dad would be away on work. They knew that if he knew what they were up to, he wouldn't approve, and this would also give Elbert the time he needed to get his plan in place.

Chapter 17

On Sunday morning, Elbert attended Mass at St. James Catholic Church with Jack's family, and he was also allowed to attend CCD class with Jack prior to the service. Elbert had already completed his Catholic confirmation, but he found Mrs. Delaney, the class instructor, to be very motivated. She really seemed to enjoy teaching the students.

While the students discussed and answered their study questions, Elbert ruminated as to why the miracles that Jesus had performed in feeding the hungry and in healing the infirm, or in forgiving us for our sins, couldn't have extended to protecting his father from death. Would Jesus forgive him for feeling as though he'd forsaken him and his mother? He secretly wished Mrs. Delaney could lead a discussion that resolved his feelings of anger and resentment towards God, but then when Mrs. Delaney reminded the students that Jesus taught us to honor our mother and father, Elbert considered that perhaps he would need to honor his father's death by trying to live a life that would have made his dad proud. As he would have lived.

After Mass, Mr. O'Malley drove the family to a small hotel restaurant, where Elbert, Jack, and Brendan all ordered a stack of pancakes with a side order of bacon. Jack laughed as Brendan's plate overflowed from a generous pour of maple syrup that his brother insisted on applying himself. Mr. and Mrs. O'Malley ordered coffee along with eggs and toast.

After brunch, the family returned home, where the boys changed into their swim trunks and rode off on their bicycles to the pool, where they would enjoy the afternoon, promising to be home in time for dinner. As they crossed Annandale Road, Elbert looked to his left at the private entrance to the house in the woods. From about a quarter of a mile away, it would have been nearly invisible to most, but what caught his eye was the blinking turn signal of a tow truck that was about to enter the driveway.

After signing in at the pool entrance, Brendan immediately went off to find his friends from swim team. Standing six feet tall, his chest, shoulders, and arms perfectly developed, muscular without being bulky, Elbert looked more like Jack's uncle than he did his cousin, and Jack noticed several people staring at Elbert as they placed their sneakers, towels, and tee shirts on the pair of lounge chairs they picked out next to those of Dana and Judy. After introducing his cousin to Judy, Jack smiled at the way Judy kept staring at Elbert while she brushed her hair, clearly unable to believe he was only thirteen years old.

Jack and Elbert went directly to the high diving board. Jack started off with a flip while Elbert started off with an inward dive that ended with Elbert's perfect entrance into the water. Jack was afraid to do inward dives because he was always concerned that he might end up hitting the board, but his cousin made it look effortless.

Jack remembered going on a fishing and hiking trip with Uncle Bert and his cousin a few years earlier, and how Elbert would do inward dives and somersaults from a rock about twenty feet above the water at Brush Creek Falls. Jack could only muster the courage to jump stiff-legged off the rock, hoping that the water below was deep enough to prevent him from touching the bottom, and he marveled at the strength in Elbert's fingers as he forced them into the smallest of a mountain's crevices to anchor himself as he climbed high upon dangerous rock formations near the swimming hole. Jack did his best to keep up on the hikes and climbed the easier segments of rocks that Uncle Bert would allow him to attempt, but he knew deep down that his cousin had physical abilities that he would never possess.

The boys did several more dives at the pool, then decided to take a break. After purchasing a couple of orange-flavored popsicles, the boys headed over to their chairs, and were drying off in the sun when the Talbot twins walked by wearing identical blue-and-red-striped one-pieces.

"Hi Jack, who's your friend?" asked Anna.

"Hi Anna," said Jack. "This is my cousin, Elbert. He's visiting from West Virginia." Then facing his cousin, he said, "Elbert, this is Anna and Danielle Talbot."

Elbert smiled. "Hi girls," he said before quickly returning to devouring his popsicle.

"Elbert is a funny name. Sort of like Elvis!" chimed in Danielle.

"We'll see you later, Jack. Nice meeting you, Elbert," said Anna as she smiled at Jack and walked away.

After the twins were gone, Dana looked at Jack. "I think Anna likes you," she said.

Jack raised his eyebrows and tilted his head towards Dana, refusing to take the bait.

Changing the subject, he asked, "Elbert, do you think we should get another popsicle?"

"Best idea I've heard all day," he replied.

As the boys walked towards the concession stand, Dana smiled and began singing. "Jack and Anna, sitting in a tree, K-I-SS-ING. First comes love, then comes marriage. Then comes baby in the baby carriage!"

Jack looked back, shaking his head at Dana as she and Judy gave each other high fives in mock celebration.

*   *   *

After gathering up Brendan's things, the boys left the pool and jumped on their bikes to return home. As they approached Annandale Road to cross, Elbert again glanced at the roped-off driveway. This time, he watched as the familiar Ford Falcon slowly pulled around the side of the chain and turned out on the road, heading in their direction. As the car approached, he noticed a stocky man driving with thick blonde hair stuffed under a New York Mets baseball cap, and a passenger next to him with dark hair and a sour-looking disposition. Both men were smoking cigarettes with the windows rolled down. As the car passed by the boys, Elbert was certain that the passenger was the man he and Jack had seen in the woods with the gun, so he looked down at the ground to make sure that he wouldn't be recognized.

Back at the O'Malley house, Elbert told Jack what he had seen, and asked him to change into his running clothes and tell his parents they were going for a quick pre-dinner run.

Chapter 18

Jimmy Szymanski was in an unusually bad mood. His hangover from downing more than a fifth of bourbon the previous evening had created a splitting headache that was causing his temples to sound a painful drumbeat with each pulse of blood that his heart produced. He knew that the only cure for this type of hangover was pouring another few gulps of whiskey down his throat to numb his brain. He tossed the cigarette he was smoking out of George's car window. Normally, a cigarette gave him a bit of relief from his hangover, but today it only made him feel more nauseous.

Jimmy was particularly unhappy with George DiCandilo. George hadn't arrived home until after 7:00 p.m. the night before, and instead of bringing hamburgers to cook on the grill, the unreliable bastard had only brought more bourbon and cigarettes, which meant that Jimmy had to dine on Jim Beam and a stale bag of pretzel rods. George's excuse for the lack of food was that when he met with Fast Eddie yesterday, he could only come up with $5,000, which meant that George could only pass half of the bills to the pimp and drug dealer that he had hoped to circulate.

George told him that he'd nearly pissed his pants when Fast Eddie pulled his gun and pointed it at his head, ordering him to hand over the full bag containing $30,000 in counterfeit notes. The only thing that George could think of saying to the thug was to think twice. If he took the extra $15,000, that was the end of the line for Fast Eddie. His well would have officially dried up, and sooner or later, the people George worked for would be hunting him. According to George, Fast Eddie smiled, tucked his gun into his pants, and said that he was "just testing" him. But when George told Tony about what happened, he hit the roof.

"If that weaselly, street punk ever tries to pull this type of crap again, cut him off completely," Mancini told him. "And since you weren't able to deliver on what you promised . . . you and Jimmy aren't getting paid for the week. I'm going to give you thirty bucks for booze and gas, but if I'm not getting my full share then you and Jimmy aren't getting anything. My deal was that you need to clear ten thousand in cash before I pay you and Jimmy your cut."

*   *   *

Anthony Mancini sat on a couch in the women's dress department of the upscale Woodward and Lothrop department store in Falls Church, Virginia. His wife needed a new outfit for a fundraising event that they were attending, and she wanted her husband's opinion on whether the champagne-colored gown looked better with her auburn hair and diamond necklace and earrings, or whether the simple, tight-fitting black dress with black heels and pearl necklace was more flattering.

After noting the lower price tag on the black dress, Tony smiled and said, "No one will be able to take their eyes off of you if you go with this one."

However, Sydnee would have been stunningly beautiful in any outfit she might have chosen. Tony knew when he married her three years ago that she wasn't choosing him for his good looks and charming personality. She was fifteen years younger than him, and was looking for a man who could provide her with the same type of lifestyle that her late father, a successful Washington lobbyist, had always afforded her.

Tony's first marriage had ended badly. His lack of fidelity had been well documented by his ex-wife's private detective, resulting in a costly settlement and alimony agreement. That, along with a downturn in the printing business, was continuing to cause his cash flow to hemorrhage at an unsustainable rate.

Tony never wanted to be in the printing business. But when his father died suddenly, he had no choice but to step into the role as President of Mancini Printing. And while unsatisfying to him professionally, it did provide him with a six-figure income that was sufficient to build a beautiful home in Mount Vernon with a view of the Potomac. His ex-wife now owned that, so today he and Sydnee lived in a small but well-appointed home in an upscale community in McLean that carried a mortgage, as did his small high-rise condo in Sarasota, FL.

Tony understood business, but had never considered himself an artist, so he delegated the printing to printers, people who could toil for hours with the art and science of photographic negatives, creating copper and aluminum plates, and painstakingly making adjustments to prepare the press to produce its printed product.

Anthony was the client-facing dealmaker. His clients were large and mid-sized corporations who outsourced their point-of-sale marketing materials to Mancini Printing, because Mancini provided the finest quality product and the best comprehensive service in the Mid-Atlantic region. Mancini accepted no government printing contracts because they "didn't give a shit about quality or service," and instead only seemed to want a vendor who could produce the most for the least.

But over the past two years it seemed that many of his corporate clients were treating his thirty-day invoice statements as suggestions rather than expectations. A number of clients had begun to negotiate smaller printing contracts, all in spite of the fact the nation's economy was strong in most sectors.

Tony saw that the future of his business would not be in printing. New ink-jet capability that was being developed would improve quality and lower costs, making it much easier for his corporate clients to produce the majority of their point-of-sale material in-house. Tony had created an affiliated business, Synergy Consulting, as a marketing consulting firm to help companies plot out their marketing strategies for the future and to help them deliver the marketing materials that they would need to meet those strategies whether they were printed by Mancini Printing or not.

With a little luck, Synergy would start generating the revenues that he'd projected, and with the consulting contracts he'd recently closed with a large defense contractor and with a life insurance company, Tony was confident that he would soon be able to rely on Synergy to contribute more than half of his revenue and more than two-thirds of his profits to his bottom line.

Then he could shut down the venture with Jimmy and George. He knew that if it went on much longer they would inevitably screw up and get caught. All greedy counterfeiters were eventually busted, and he knew that he was stretching the limits already. If things continued to go as planned with Synergy, within a few months he could be rid of Jimmy and George for good.

* * *

Fear made its home in the pit of Jack's stomach as he agreed to accompany Elbert on his mission to scout out the barn while the two men were away. Once Elbert saw the men drive away in the Ford Falcon, he couldn't be dissuaded from taking advantage of the opportunity. A sense of guilt made matters even worse for Jack, as he had lied to his parents about going for a quick run before dinner.

"Well, we will be running, so it's only bending the truth," reminded Elbert.

Elbert's plan was straightforward. He had thought of a way that he could enter the barn, but Jack would need to remain outside to stand guard. If he heard a vehicle pull into the driveway he needed to shoot pellets against the walls of the barn or its door to alert him that it was time to leave.

After retrieving the pellet gun and ammo from the tree fort, Jack assumed his position behind a row of bushes that provided ample cover, while at the same time giving him access to the barn and a view of the driveway. He said a quick prayer, asking God to let them get through this event unscathed, and promised to lead a life free of sin if God could give them a free pass today.

Tired of being afraid. Tired of the embarrassment. Tired of letting those who care about him down. These were the feelings that Jack dealt with whenever a moment of truth faced him. Jack always felt a strong sense of empathy for those he encountered. It endeared him in many ways to others and helped him to fit in. The downside of empathy, for Jack, was an extreme sense of self-consciousness about how he was fitting in and how others were perceiving him. He preferred to be low key and avoid being the center of attention. Yes, being accepted by others, being liked was something that Jack had to admit was important to him.

Why did Elbert seem to be impervious to these fears? What set him apart from everyone else in that regard? He seemed to possess, if not empathy, at least a degree of sensitivity for the feelings of others. But never could Jack ever recall a moment when Elbert relied on the acceptance of others to dictate his behavior or his actions, or more importantly, his self-worth.

Perhaps this explained the unimaginable pain that he must be feeling having lost his father. Uncle Bert and his father, Grandpa Elbert Justice, were built of the same quiet confidence that had been passed on to Elbert. Both were pillars of their community for their accomplishments and for the respectful manner in which they treated everyone they encountered. Would it change Elbert to no longer have those examples in his life to learn from?

Self-confidence and humble respect for others without the need for acceptance. Were these traits that must be inherited from one generation to the next or could they be developed through observation and practice? Were they within reach or simply questions to ponder, and in doing so diminish his own self-confidence even further? Jack admired his cousin, he loved him like a brother. But was the large shadow that he cast an image he couldn't live up to, or a hint of what he would become?

He watched Elbert scamper through the woods and quickly disappear behind the barn, undoubtedly with a purpose in mind. A few seconds later he saw his cousin rise from beyond the roof, shimmying up a tree like a caterpillar escaping upward from a fire below. Reaching a branch a few feet higher than the roof, Elbert swung from the branch, quietly dropping himself on the warm tin surface.

Elbert quickly found the vent in the middle of the roof, using his knife to loosen the four screws holding the vent to its enclosure. He then removed the vent and peered into the barn. The smell of gasoline filled his senses as he took in the dusty garage of unattended machinery, plants, and storage for odds and ends.

Directly below the vent, Elbert found a spot on the floor where he could land, and swiftly lowered himself from the ledge of the vent, dropping nearly fifteen feet to the dirt floor below. As he lifted himself from the ground, a three-foot-long black snake, likely in search of water or a rodent, scurried underneath an old tractor.

Elbert moved within seconds to the barn door and pulled the lock mechanism, unlocking the door without opening it. He then moved to the inner door to the office, but found it locked. Looking through the window in the door, he saw, illuminated by the sharp rays of late-afternoon sunlight shining from the front window, what appeared to him to be a printing machine resting on the table within.

Pulling two bobby pins that he had "borrowed" from Aunt Kathleen and configured in a manner that his Dad had once taught him, he slid the pins into the lock. After adjusting his movements and pressure for a few moments, he was able to pick the lock and enter the office. But just as Elbert closed the door behind him, he heard the pinging sound of Jack shooting pellets off the walls of the barn. It was time to leave.

He glanced quickly around the office before returning to the main barn, exiting through the barn door and closing it behind him. He ran quickly into the bushes and followed Jack, who sprinted at a faster pace than even he could match. Reaching the tree fort, Jack sat engulfed in awe and adrenaline. Elbert had climbed up the rope ladder just as the Ford Falcon pulled to a stop in front of the house.

Chapter 19

George and Jimmy felt satisfied with how their meeting had gone with Fast Eddie, who'd agreed to meet with them in the parking lot of a closed liquor store, directly across Key Bridge in Georgetown. Jimmy insisted on accompanying George for the meeting, and on bringing his gun. Just to let Eddie know that they weren't screwing around.

They had made it clear to Eddie that their boss wasn't pleased with the stunt he tried to pull at the last exchange. That they would convey this adequately was the promise George had given to Tony. But the remaining agenda items that George and Jimmy shared with Eddie were certainly not part of the script that had been shared with Mancini. Jimmy and George asked Eddie point blank if he could handle $500,000 in tens and twenties in exchange for $60,000 in cash. About twelve cents on the dollar was a lot better than the thirty-cent deal Eddie had been getting, so when he asked why they suddenly wanted to cut him a sweeter deal, George answered that it was a "quantity discount." Eddie would need to work together with his cousin Dead-Eye from Baltimore, but he would have his answer for them tomorrow evening.

As George and Jimmy returned home with pork chops to cook on the grill, they felt confident that they would soon be on a boat off the coast of Mexico, with a new life and more than $50,000 in their pockets to start their new, healthier existence. Away from Anthony Mancini and Fast Eddie. A life without printing. Nothing to do each day but to cruise on their boat and fish for their food. They both agreed that life in Mexico would be exactly what they needed and deserved. They would give up smoking and the booze. OK, maybe they could drink a few Mexican beers, but no hard stuff, and the occasional cigar might be OK, too. Oh yes, their lives were about to take a turn. And most certainly it would be a turn for the better. That was for sure.

Chapter 20

Monday morning turned out to be the most beautiful day of the summer. The temperature was warm but there didn't seem to be a single ounce of humidity in the air. Jack looked in the sky and was pleased. He picked up the *Washington Post* that was lying on the driveway and noticed that the weather forecast, published on the front page, noted temperatures in the 80s for the day with almost no humidity and a zero chance of precipitation. Perfect weather conditions for the Pirates' key game of the season. A win tonight against the Cardinals would clinch the league championship. A loss would require the two teams to play another game against each other as a tie-breaker.

"Hi Jack," yelled Dana from across the street.

Jack walked across the cul-de-sac and asked Dana what her plans were for the day.

"I don't really have any plans, but I'll be around if you and Elbert want to hang out," she responded.

Jack told Dana about his baseball game at 5:30 p.m. and invited her to attend with his family.

"That sounds like fun," she said, "you know they sell snow cones at the park!"

"Good, I'll tell my mom and dad to expect you. They'll be leaving at around five, so you can ride to the game with them and Elbert and Brendan. I'll be riding to the game with Coach Russell to get there early for our pre-game practice."

As Jack returned to his house, Dana said with a smile, "I hope you do well tonight, Jack. If you hit a home run, maybe I'll give you that kiss I know you've been hoping for!"

Jack couldn't hide his grin. Boy, he thought to himself for the second time this morning, it really was a beautiful day!

For most of the day Jack caught up on his reading and knocked out his exercise routine. Then he and Elbert accompanied his Dad on a couple of trips to the hardware store, where his father needed to pick up items to replace a broken window pane that Brendan had accidentally shattered when a rock he had thrown to scare a squirrel had missed its mark by a wide margin. During their second trip to the store, Mr. O'Malley pulled into the nearby McDonald's drive-in, where they ordered cheeseburgers and fries to bring home for lunch for the whole family.

Elbert volunteered to help his uncle with the window replacement project, while Jack caught up on current events as reported in the *Post*.

Field number one at Annandale Recreational Park was always the favorite amongst Little League players in Fairfax County. The outfield fence was draped with a green plastic liner that clearly delineated the fence from the outlying area. In fact, a home run over the left-field fence could easily reach the concession stand that stood beyond. But what really separated field number one from the two other fields was the fact that advertisers had paid to have their corporate signs posted on the outfield fence. Parents in the stands could be reminded how the Capitol Ford dealership could make their family "The Pride of the Neighborhood," and how the Macon Brothers Plumbing Company could provide "Clear Sailing to their Pipes, Regardless of the Season." Even the Fairfax County Board of

Supervisors paid for a sign promising a "Grand Slam" of a legislative year to their constituents.

To a group of eleven- and twelve-year-olds, a stadium with a fence and signage on the outfield wall, along with an infield and outfield that looked as green as an Irish landscape, felt like heaven. But to Jack, what made field number one most special was that in a small black elevated enclosure, behind the home plate backstop, stood a booth on stilts that housed the game announcer. The announcer helped provide an added sense of importance to the game. Introducing the starting lineups, and each of the batters. Calling the balls and strikes, and from time to time, adding extra color commentary to the importance of the moment in a game.

Art McNeeley had announced all of the games that Jack had attended at Annandale Park. His love of the sport, his baritone voice, and his knowledge of the game always added an extra element of excitement to a sport that was already great at its very foundation, elevating it even higher with his oratory.

As the Pirates finished their fielding and batting practice and jogged to the dugout for their last-minute instructions from Coach Russell, Jack looked to the stands behind his side of the field. There he saw his father, mother, Brendan, Elbert, and Dana all waving, their faces smiling in anticipation. Even Mr. and Mrs. Atkins had showed up for the game, smiling with pride that seemed equal to that of his family's. And although he knew he wasn't there to cheer him on, he even spotted Gary Saunders in the stands, sitting next to Kenny Tucker.

Allen Tallman was the starting pitcher for the Cardinals. Tallman was known as the best pitcher in the entire Fairfax league. At 5'10" and 130 pounds, he was larger than most of the players on the field, and his athleticism was superior to virtually anyone in the league. The Cardinals had a solid team, coached by Jim Dunnington. They hit well, played solid defense, and their pitching was regarded as their key strength.

Jack had known Allen Tallman since he was in the first grade. Although they grew up in different neighborhoods, Tallman attended

St. James Catholic Church with Jack and the two often attended the same CCD classes on Sundays. Jack thought Allen was a good guy. Great in sports, yet he didn't make others feel inferior. He always treated Jack like a friend. And as a result, for some unknown reason, Jack felt comfortable facing him in their games, despite his skill and reputation as a hurler.

In the first inning, Tallman struck out the first two Pirates before Trey Clendenon connected on a fastball, ripping it down the left-field line for a stand-up double. Randy Russell batted cleanup and managed a walk on a borderline pitch, which Coach Dunnington clearly disagreed with.

"Batting fifth for the Pirates is right fielder Jack O'Malley," Mr. McNeely announced.

With runners on first and second, Jack stepped into the batter's box. He looked to Coach Russell, who was standing on third base, to see if he was being given a sign to either bunt or take a pitch. With no signal, Jack knew he was free to swing away.

Tallman delivered a curve that came dangerously close to clipping Jack's left leg, but he narrowly avoided it by pulling his leg backwards. The pitch escaped the Cardinals catcher, allowing both runners to advance to second and third base.

"Ball One," the umpire bellowed, and Jack knew that Allen would want to get the next pitch over the plate, so he prepared for a fastball.

The fastball seemed to come in slow motion to Jack, even though he knew it had been thrown harder than any Mr. Russell had pitched during batting practice sessions. Jack waited until he was sure, and then shifted his weight and turned his shoulders to make sure that his contact delivered its maximum force. Once the bat struck the ball, Jack knew it was solidly hit, with the ball bouncing off the outfield turf and over the Capitol Ford sign in center field.

With his ground-rule double, Jack was standing on second base, with runners Clendenon and Russell having scored. Jack kicked the clay from his cleats as he glanced at the stands and saw his fan club cheering wildly along with the entire Pirates section. Even Brendan was giving out high fives to everyone sitting within range. No doubt, Jack thought to himself, Brendan was letting everyone know that he had been working with me on my hitting deficiencies during the offseason.

Paul Hassler pitched solidly in the first and second innings for the Pirates, striking out three Cardinals while retiring the three other batters with ground balls that were all solidly defended by the Pirates infield. This allowed his team to maintain their 2-0 lead into the third inning.

In the Pirates half of the third inning, Randy Russell walked after tiring Tallman by fouling off four pitches before the pitcher tossed his final curve into the dirt to put him on base. As Jack came to the plate again, he felt a sense of confidence that had eluded him in nearly every game that he could recall.

Jack loved the game of baseball, despite the fact that for the six years that he had participated in organized leagues he had an overall batting average that was sub-.200. And when you added in his weak defensive skills, it was somewhat unfathomable to recognize what Coach Russell saw in him when he allowed him to assume a starting position on a contending team.

Jack wore the number nine in honor of his favorite New York Yankee, Roger Maris. Maris clubbed a record sixty-one home runs for the Yanks in 1961, breaking the record of the immortal Babe Ruth. Yet Maris was never popular with the fans in New York or elsewhere for that matter. Jack was drawn to him because he viewed him as the underdog, the understudy to the ever-popular media darling, Mickey Mantle.

Jack loved Mantle nearly as much, but something about Maris resonated in him. How could a player whom fans disliked and whom sportswriters disdained go out each day and not be resentful of the way he was being treated? But perhaps that was what drove him to prove to the fans, the media, and to the world that, damn it, he would show them what he was capable of doing. And he did.

Most of Jack's teammates liked him. They generally viewed him as a smart and affable teammate, and as someone who always tried hard. But in a game situation where a win or a loss was on the line, Jack was aware that most of his teammates would have preferred if Jack asked to be benched, feigning a pulled muscle or some imaginary stomach ailment.

But for now, during a key game in the Pirates season, he was the game leader for his team in RBIs, even if it was based on only one at-bat. Walking into the batter's box, Jack looked at his friend Allen Tallman and nodded affirmatively that he was ready.

Tallman fired a fastball that touched the outside corner of the plate for strike one. Jack knew, before the at-bat, that he wanted to look at the first pitch to help gauge the speed, observe the pitcher's motion, and watch the movement of the ball. The next pitch was another fastball, this time delivered inside towards the inner portion of the plate. Jack reacted late and was lucky to foul the pitch above the Cardinals dugout on the first-base side of the field.

With a count of no balls and two strikes, Jack realized that he needed to expect Tallman to throw him nothing easy to hit for the next few pitches, and in fact, the next pitch bounced off the dirt in front of home plate for ball one, while the following pitch sailed high above Jack's eye level, tying the count at two and two.

On the fifth pitch of the at-bat, Tallman threw a fastball that caught too much of the center of the plate, allowing Jack to strike it with the head of his bat, belting it into the gap in right-center field. The Cardinals right fielder recovered the ball at the fence but fumbled it sufficiently before his throw, allowing Russell to score from first base.

Jack stood at second base for the second time in the game, with the score now 3-0, and with the Pirates fans all standing and cheering loudly. Tallman looked back at second base, his eyes filled with disappointment. He never thought that Jack could produce enough bat speed to produce such a solid hit off his fastball, but damn if he hadn't done it twice in the past three innings. He liked Jack, but he sure didn't like him enough to want to see him hurt the Cardinals' chances in this big game.

Jack felt a sense of nervousness standing on second. It wasn't as though he had a lot of experience knocking in runners, especially against a pitcher who was considered the best in the league. But oh how he wanted to appear calm and confident. Jack wondered if anyone in the stands could sense that his legs were shaking. But deep down inside, he knew they could not.

In the fifth inning, the Cardinals rallied to score four runs off Hassler. The left fielder for the Cardinals, Bobby Dunnington, appeared to be a man playing a child's game. Standing at 5'10" and weighing close to 150 pounds, Dunnington appeared much older than his actual age of twelve. His dark black hair and the facial hair on his face was evident to every player on the Pirates. To Jack and his teammates, he resembled a forty-year-old salesman who had been traveling for three days, without the benefit of a shower or a shave. The stubble on his face was the envy of every boy on the Pirates, all of whom could only dream of needing to shave.

Dunnington's grand slam over the left-field fence cleared not only the playing field, but traveled another forty feet to career off the roof of the concession stand. The stands on the Cardinals side of the field cheered as big Bobby Dunnington lumbered around the bases and touched home plate, giving his team a four to three lead.

Summer league baseball games were six-inning affairs, so the opportunity for the Pirates to regain the lead, or to at least tie the game, rested in their ability to produce one or more runs in the top half of the sixth inning. The manager for the Cardinals, Bobby Dunnington's father, decided to make a pitching change, bringing his son to the mound to relieve Allen Tallman.

In reality, Dunnington was not as good a pitcher as Tallman. His fastball was a little slower, although it was fast. His curve ball wasn't as sharp or as sneaky, but it was adequate. And Bobby Dunnington was a wilder pitcher than Tallman. But, for a nervous, unconfident hitter like Jack, wildness sent shivers up his spine. More importantly, the sight of a twelve-year-old with three-day stubble on his face and a body that was as big as his father's was quite disconcerting.

The first two at-bats for the Pirates did not go well. Leftfielder Brett McDaniel swatted blindly at the first three pitches that Dunnington threw, all fastballs, without making contact. Trey Clendenon was at least able to make contact on a fastball, but could only manage a pop-up that landed comfortably in Dunnington's glove near the pitcher's mound.

When Randy Russell approached the plate, the Pirates fans cheered him on, despite their feeling that perhaps this game had slipped out of their hands.

"Watch the ball, make solid contact, get on base," Coach Russell yelled from the third-base box.

On the first pitch from Dunnington, a fastball, Russell slapped a hard grounder that slipped through the gap between the shortstop and the third baseman for a base hit. The Pirates fans all cheered in hopes that a rally was still possible.

Jack approached the batter's box and peeked at Dunnington, a player who he'd seen before, but didn't know personally. *He really does have a beard,* he thought, as he dug his cleats into position and nodded to the pitcher. The first pitch from Dunnington was wild, thrown a foot above the catcher, who ran to retrieve it near the back stop. The wild pitch allowed Russell to reach second base, thus putting him in scoring position if Jack could manage a base hit.

The next pitch was a fastball that caught the outside corner. Jack watched it without swinging, just to gauge the speed. Dunnington's size intimidated Jack, making all of his pitches appear faster to him than anything he'd seen from Tallman. But in reality, Dunnington actually threw at a slightly slower velocity than the Cardinals starter.

The next pitch was a fastball down the middle, but a little high. Jack swung hard but was only able to catch a piece of the ball, fouling it back over the back-stop for strike two.

On the next pitch, Jack saw the ball heading for his left ear. Afraid that he was about to be beaned, he stepped his front foot outside of the box, turned his head down and away from the pitch and ducked away from the plate. But from his right eye, he could see the catcher receive the pitch in his glove behind the plate.

"Strike," the umpire yelled.

The game was over. Jack had fallen victim to a well-thrown curve ball that, to Jack, appeared to be heading towards his face, when in fact, it was bending back towards the plate. Had he kept his concentration on the ball, had he not bailed out and turned away, he might have better identified the curve and reacted to it. But he didn't.

From the most glorious game of his life, to perhaps his most embarrassing. All within a matter of minutes. Jack lacked the courage to make eye contact with any of his friends or family in the stands. He quietly hurried back to the dugout, collecting his glove as Coach Russell consoled his team.

"Tough game. We have practice tomorrow at 4 p.m., and tell your parents that the tie-breaker playoff game against the Cardinals will be on Saturday morning at ten."

As Jack walked to join his family for their ride home, Gary Saunders approached him with a snow cone in his hand, alongside Kenny Tucker. "Hey Jack, tough game. Remember, you can't bale out if you want to hit the curve ball. If you want me to teach you how to keep your head in on a curve, come by tomorrow and I'll show you."

Dana stepped between Gary and Jack. "You don't know what you're talking about. You've never played baseball, and the only time I've seen you play softball or whiffle ball - you were terrible!"

"You'd better stay away from me, Dana. I wasn't even talking to you. And just so you know," said Gary nervously, "my mother told me that if you punch me, even though you're a girl, it's OK for me to defend myself and punch you back."

Dana smiled at Gary, looked at Jack, then ran towards Gary. With both of her arms extended and all of her momentum, she pushed him in his chest, knocking him, and his snow cone, backwards onto the grassy turf.

As she turned to walk away, she shot out, "Fine. Did your mother tell you what to do if I pushed you?"

The ride home from the ballpark wasn't the celebration that Jack had hoped for. Both teams were now tied for the league title, and the playoff game between them would end up deciding the season's champion. Elbert reminded Jack that he was responsible for all three runs that the Pirates scored in the game. Jack's dad pointed out that Dunnington's curve was very well thrown, and that he shouldn't feel ashamed that it fooled him. "Give him credit, Jack. He threw an unhittable pitch."

Even Brendan couldn't feel comfortable piling on top of Jack's misery. "You were the only player on the Pirates who hit two doubles today, Jack. So, the reason why your team lost has a lot more to do with the fact that the other players on your team weren't able to get their share of hits to support what you were able to do."

"Thanks everyone," said Jack. "I know you're all trying to cheer me up. I doubt there is anything that you can say that will make me feel like I didn't choke on his curve, but I appreciate everyone's efforts. It's just that I thought I was getting better at looking for the curve ball."

Dana, wanting to break the tension, asked, "When was the last time you had two doubles and knocked in three runners in a single game?"

Jack realized that the answer to her question was that he never had, and that regardless of how it had ended, he'd just completed the most productive game of his life. Before he could say anything, Dana leaned towards his ear and whispered, "And if you're lucky you still might get that kiss."

While the pain of his strikeout didn't completely evaporate, Jack smiled even more than he wanted to for the remainder of the drive home.

Chapter 21

On Tuesday, Jack awakened and hopped out of bed at 7:00 am. Purposely, he walked to the dining room, where his mother was drinking a cup of coffee and reading the newspaper.

"Did Dad leave already?"

"Yes, he left at about 5:30 this morning. He and his team of agents had to board a plane that is probably taking off right about now from Andrews Air Force base," she replied.

Jack was disappointed with himself for not waking up early enough to say goodbye to his father. He walked into the kitchen and poured himself a bowl of Raisin Bran with milk and returned to the table.

"Did Dad tell you where he was headed?"

"Well, I only know that their first stop will be in Chicago, but after that, they will be moving all around the country. In Chicago, at least, I know that they are working on advance protection details for the upcoming Democratic National Convention."

Jack ate his cereal and asked his mom if he could look at the sports page while she was reading the national news section of the *Post*.

"Today, I'll be taking your brother to swim practice, and afterwards, he and I will be going to Dr. Clements' office for our dental check-ups. Will you and Elbert be OK while we're out?" she asked.

"Sure, don't worry about us. We'll be hanging out here most of the day, and maybe go scouting around in the woods if Gary will let us near his tree fort."

"Well, after last evening's dust-up with Dana, I wouldn't expect Gary to be in a very good mood." His mother paused, not wanting to add that Gary Saunders never seemed to be in a good mood, unless he was bossing someone around.

Jack admired his mom for her positive and productive persona, but he knew she worried whenever his father was away on protective duty. In a year where one candidate was already killed, it only made her more nervous that her husband and his fellow agents could find themselves in harm's way. Having to take care of three children and manage a household was enough for anyone to handle without the added stress of her husband's occupation.

After breakfast, Jack finished reading the paper, while Brendan awakened, ate breakfast, and headed out with his mom for swim practice. Elbert slept until eight, and ate two bowls of Raisin Bran along with two pieces of toast with peanut butter before he looked at Jack and said, "Are you ready to go?"

"Where do you want to go?" asked Jack.

"We need to do some reconnaissance. Let's try to find a position where we can learn more about what those guys are doing in that barn."

"You know, Elbert," replied Jack, "I've been thinking, and at this point we've been doing a lot of snooping around, but we still aren't sure that they are doing anything wrong or illegal. I know you have this suspicion that they are printing counterfeit money. But think about it - just because you think they have a printing machine and some currency-quality paper doesn't make them criminals. I mean, have you looked at those two guys? Do they look like successful counterfeiters to you? If these are just a couple of innocent guys who like to drink a lot, the only people who are breaking the law are you and me. For trespassing on their property."

"Well Jack, if they aren't doing anything wrong, we should soon be able to figure that out and we can drop it," said Elbert.

"OK, and what if we find out that they are making counterfeit money? We're just kids. So, will you at least agree that we should contact the police or the Secret Service?" pleaded Jack.

"Absolutely," assured Elbert. "Once we know what they are up to we can either drop it, or we can call in the police to take over from there."

Chapter 22

Elbert led Jack to the tree fort and the boys climbed the rope ladder, with Elbert using his binoculars to see if he could spot any movement near the barn. After noticing that the barn's office door was closed and the lights inside appeared to be turned off, he assumed that the men had not yet awakened and left the house. Elbert suggested that they move closer to the barn to get a better look at the surroundings, but just as the boys were exiting the tree fort, Gary Saunders arrived with Kenny Tucker.

Gary shouted, "Jack, you know better than to be using my tree fort without my permission. I know that you have your cousin visiting and all, but this is my tree fort and when you decided to not help me finish with the construction, I always knew that you would regret it." Gary paused before adding, "There are consequences for being a quitter, Jack, and the consequence in this case is that the tree fort is off-limits to you, unless you first get my permission."

Jack couldn't stand to hear one of Gary's lectures, but in this instance he knew that he and Elbert had been caught red-handed exiting the fort, so there was no use in trying to talk his way out of it.

"I understand, Gary. I just thought that Elbert would appreciate the fine work that you put into building it. But don't worry, it won't happen again," Jack said, wanting the conversation to end, even though he knew he was lying. Deep down he had little doubt that he and Elbert would be visiting the fort again in the future.

As Gary and Kenny climbed up into the fort, Elbert and Jack walked towards the creek. "Come on, Jack," Elbert said loudly. "Let's see if we can catch some frogs near the creek."

Knowing that Gary and Kenny were now in the tree fort forced Elbert to find an alternative position for them to conduct their surveillance of the barn. He wanted to avoid being in view of Gary or Kenny, realizing that this would only spark their curiosity.

As the boys crossed over the creek, Elbert glanced back at the fort to try to approximate its field of vision. He realized that Gary and Kenny probably didn't have binoculars, but if he or Jack were to hide behind the ferns near the entrance of the barn, they might, still be visible from the fort.

As they moved towards some bushes and trees to the left of the barn, Elbert found a tree that he could climb to a height of about twenty feet above the ground, with branches that were well protected by foliage. The branches offered a thick platform where Elbert could lay without being seen clearly from either the house or from the driveway should the men appear.

He suggested that Jack should retreat about fifteen yards from the barn, behind rows of holly bushes, and find a spot where he could lie on the leaf-covered ground. From there he would be able to see movement from the barn or the driveway, and overhear most of the communication.

Elbert advised, "If I'm spotted by the men while I'm up in the tree, I will drop quickly to the ground and run up the creek line towards the neighborhood that is next to yours. You should grab a rock, and if they chase after me, you can throw it towards the trashcans near the house. That should distract them enough to give us both a few seconds' head start. Then, high-tail it in the opposite direction and head back towards Mr. Atkins' yard. I will work my way back to your neighborhood and will rejoin you at your house as soon as I can get there."

Jack hurried over to the bushes and looked for a good place to lie and be difficult to spot, and found a rock about half the size of a baseball for him to use as a diversion, in the event it was needed. He watched in amazement as his cousin easily scaled the tree and moved into position on the thick branch that extended near the front left side of the barn's office. The strength of Elbert's grip and his ability to use his feet as if they were webbed simply defied anything that Jack could conceive possible.

The boys remained in their positions for more than ten minutes before hearing any movement. Jack had endured the sounds of insects flying near the bushes, birds chirping, and even the occasional murmur of muffled voices from the tree fort about sixty yards behind him. But the movement he was hearing now was definitely coming from the front of the house. One of the men had exited through the front door and stepped off the porch, holding a cup of coffee. It was the same tall man they had seen with the gun in the woods. He was wearing a pair of white painter pants and a white tee-shirt along with a pair of black work boots. He tossed the remains of his coffee into the gravel and set his mug on the porch railing.

Jimmy Szymanski lit a Chesterfield and took a drag, followed by a long coughing burst that lasted for nearly twenty seconds, causing him to nearly double over. As painful as it was, Jimmy realized that these early morning coughing spells were a necessary phase for him to clear his lungs of the poisons that had entered his body from the previous evening's abuse of liquor and tobacco. He promised himself how his health would change for the better if he and George could pull off their final act of circulating their counterfeit bills with Fast Eddie and his cousin. Then, he and George could finally head to Mexico, buy a sailboat that could sleep at least four, and begin a new life. One that was healthier and without the booze and the smoking.

After a few more drags, he tossed the butt on the gravel driveway and crushed it with the sole of his boot. He then walked towards the barn. Pulling a ring of keys from his pocket, he fumbled for the correct key before turning the lock and opening the office door. He then stepped inside to turn on the office lights and switched on the printer before leaving the building again while the printer warmed up. He took a seat on the bench and relaxed, lighting another cigarette. Elbert was close enough to the front of the barn that he could smell the smoke of the freshly lit cigarette wafting into the air.

The front door to the house opened again and the second man that Elbert had spotted previously appeared. He too was carrying a mug of coffee as he walked across the driveway towards Jimmy.

"Beautiful day, don't you think Jimmy?" George said.

Jimmy replied, "Hot and muggy if you ask me, George."

"You were so trashed last night, you probably don't recall anything I told you about my meeting with Eddie and his cousin, do you?" asked George.

"No lectures, please, about my drinking, George. I noticed that the final fifth of Jim Beam was empty on the counter, so I'm pretty sure you had your share, too," chastised Jimmy. "So how did your visit with Eddie go?"

After taking a sip of his coffee, George set the mug on the bench next to him and replied, "Well, if you think Fast Eddie scares me . . . he's nothing compared to his cousin, Dead-Eye. The guy is about 6'3" and solid muscle, with tattoos all over his massive arms. He's got a scar that runs from his left eye to his upper lip that I don't think he got from shaving. And that left eye of his; shit, I couldn't tell if he was looking at me or at Eddie. Cross-eyed as a son of a bitch."

"Does he want in on our deal?" asked Jimmy impatiently.

"Yes, he does," said George as he took a sip from his mug. "But the scary bastard made sure that he put the fear of God in me by pointing his gun at my balls. Just to make his point that if we pulled any tricks on him he would kill me, after he first shot my balls off. Hell, the guy even threatened to kill Eddie if we screwed him. And by the way, Eddie is only able to come up with ten grand, so Dead-Eye is putting up the other fifty."

"Well, I don't care how much Eddie is putting in, so long as the two can come up with the total," replied Jimmy. "Where and when do they want the trade to go down?"

"I told them to meet us at the parking lot at Lake Barcroft at 8 p.m. on Thursday," said George.

Jimmy liked the idea that they would be conducting the trade at Barcroft. Neither he nor George liked having to go to the crime-ridden section of DC where Eddie normally did business. Lake Barcroft, in the nearby suburbs, was secluded, quiet, and normally had very few people around, especially at night, except for the occasional group of teenagers smoking pot or drinking beer. "So we need to print $250k in tens and $250k in twenties, right?"

"That's the deal. How many tens did you knock out last night?" asked George.

"About a hundred sheets," Jimmy answered. "With what I did during the morning we have about 10,000 notes, cut and banded. I think I can finish up the tens by tonight. Then we can switch the plates to work on the twenties tomorrow. But today, I really hope you don't mind making a food and booze run, because we are empty in the house."

"Sure thing," said George. "I'll be meeting with Mancini at eleven, and letting him know that we should be able to meet with him again on Friday to deliver his ten grand. I'll pick up the stuff then."

"You sure you want to pay him anything? We could stiff him and give ourselves another ten G's to stash into our savings. We'd probably be sailing in Mexico before he figured out we were gone," said Jimmy, who had never fully understood why George insisted on giving Tony any of their ill-gotten proceeds.

"Yes, I'm sure. Telling Tony that we're going on a fishing trip in West Virginia for a few days, after we pay him 10k for our deal with Eddie, buys us some time to get to Mexico without him getting suspicious."

Jack could hear some, but not all, of the conversation from where he was hidden in the bushes. But from Elbert's position in the tree, he was quite sure that he could hear everything that was being said.

Regardless, he knew that he'd heard enough to know what these guys were up to. Maybe now he'd be able to convince Elbert that they should contact the police, so he wouldn't have to be hiding in bushes near men with guns, who were counterfeiting money and dealing with even worse characters, like this Fast Eddie and Dead-Eye.

As George walked back to the house, Jimmy stood and returned to the office. Elbert motioned to Jack that he would be climbing down the tree and would meet him back at his house. A few seconds later, Jack left, taking the long route through the woods, entering his neighborhood through the Goodwins' yard.

Chapter 23

Elbert ran through the woods to the adjoining neighborhood, and re-entered Jack's neighborhood through the Tucker's backyard by scaling a steep dirt hill from the base of the woods. He thought about what he wanted to tell Jack, and what he might want to keep to himself, ultimately convincing himself that he wasn't really lying to his cousin if he merely omitted some of what he'd overheard. But first he needed to find out from Jack how much of Jimmy and George's conversation he had been able to hear.

Jack and Elbert noticed that the family car was still gone, meaning Mrs. O'Malley was still out with Brendan at the dentist, so Jack led Elbert back to the backyard, where the boys sat in two patio chairs under partial shade.

"What were you able to overhear from the bushes?" asked Elbert of his cousin.

"I heard enough to know that you were right about these guys. They are counterfeiters and they are planning to unload tens and twenties that they are printing for some scary guy named Dead-Eye and another guy named Eddie. And they mentioned another guy that they are working with named Mancini, and something about Lake

Barcroft. I couldn't hear everything they said, but the guy we saw with the gun is named Jimmy and I think the stocky guy is named George," said Jack.

"Well it sounds like you pretty well heard everything," said Elbert. "I'm not sure where Mancini fits in the overall scheme, but they also mentioned going fishing in West Virginia and sailing in Mexico. I heard Jimmy say that he's already working on the tens and should be finished with them by tonight and then he could start on the twenties tomorrow."

"What did they say about Barcroft?" asked Jack.

"I couldn't hear what they were talking about," lied Elbert, "but you're right that they said something about Lake Barcroft."

"Well, I think we know enough now to contact the police or the Secret Service. We should tell my mom when she gets home, and see what she says," suggested Jack.

"We could do that," paused Elbert, "but if we act too quickly, there's a good chance that all that will happen is that they will raid the house and the barn, and if Jimmy and George have hidden their counterfeit bills, they might come up emptyhanded. Plus, the chances of them catching Eddie, Dead-Eye, or this Mancini character are highly unlikely."

"Elbert, you promised me that if we were sure that they were making counterfeit money we could contact the police. I think we're now both convinced that they are counterfeiters, so why are you resisting?" pleaded Jack.

"Come on, Jack. Think about it. Let's say we call the police. They'll come here and interview you and me and we'll tell them about Jimmy and his gun. We'll tell them about us hiding up in a tree and in the bushes and about what we think we overheard them talking about," Elbert continued, trying to convince even himself. "We don't have any actual evidence that they are printing money. For all we know, these guys could be hiding the fake money, and if the police conduct a search and come away with nothing? Then, what do you think will happen next? Two angry guys named Jimmy and George will be coming after us for trying to turn them in. Not to mention the fact that Eddie, Dead-Eye, and Mancini will never be implicated in any of this.

"But," Elbert looked at Jack, and pleaded, "I have an idea about how we can get our hands on some actual evidence, so there will be no way for these guys to weasel out of this. And then we can call the police."

Jack shook his head. "You're not giving the police enough credit. When they get a search warrant to look through the house and the barn, they will be able to look through every nook and cranny on that property. And they'll interrogate Jimmy and George until they tell them everything, including spilling the beans on Eddie, Dead-Eye, and Mancini. This isn't kid stuff, Elbert. We need adults with authority to deal with this."

Elbert knew his cousin was correct. He loved adventure and wasn't afraid to take risks, but bringing Jack into the mix, unwillingly, wasn't fair to him. "I apologize, Jack. You're right about everything. So here's all I'm asking for. This evening when you go to baseball practice, I'm going to snoop around the barn one more time. With a little luck Jimmy will be drunk again, and if I can get away with it, I'm going to try to grab at least a few of their counterfeit bills. If I can get them, great. They won't be able to deny that they made them. But if I can't, then it's OK, we'll tell your mom tomorrow or even tonight after dinner. And then she can call the authorities."

Chapter 24

Elbert waited until Jack headed for Coach Russell's house on his bike a little after three, then quickly slipped down the hill behind the Allen house and into the woods. He then crawled into the bushes near where Jack had hidden earlier in the day. From his position, he could see Jimmy working in the barn's office with the door ajar. The printer was humming, and then it stopped. Jimmy lifted pages from the press, setting them on tables in the back of the office to allow the ink to dry. Using his binoculars, Elbert could see that each sheet of printing paper seemed to contain four rows of eight counterfeit bills per page. Although it was difficult to tell for sure, it appeared that Jimmy was running the front of the bills first, then allowing the ink to dry.

As Elbert continued to watch Jimmy, it appeared that he would run each page on the front of the notes a second time, likely using a second color ink for the serial numbers and the Treasury seal. Printing, drying, printing, drying the face of the bills, and then printing and drying the back of the bills. A pretty monotonous process, he thought. "No wonder they drink so much," he whispered to himself.

While Jimmy was working, George walked into the office, collecting pages of finished prints. He quickly inspected them and carried them to the back of the office. Several minutes later another machine began its chopping and sorting sounds as the bills were cut from the sheets and collected in a tray for George to inspect and then wrap in bands of one hundred bills per pack.

Elbert could hear the men speaking but was too far away to tell what they were saying. George left the office and walked towards the house, returning quickly with two Ballantine beers in hand. Jimmy exited the office and wiped his forehead with the palm of his right hand. He lit up a cigarette and blew a ring of smoke as he grabbed the beer from George and the two sat on the bench and relaxed.

"Jimmy, I have to say - you're a damn Rembrandt. I doubt there are more than fifty people in the whole country who could tell that your bills are bogus. Hell, I've passed hundreds of them at convenience stores and gas stations and never has a single bill been questioned. The way you took the negative and magically worked it into the plate, with the slight color variations," George paused. "Well, it's just God-damned amazing."

"Stop blowing smoke up my ass, George," said Jimmy. "You're as good at this as I am, but we both know the limitations to this game. Sooner or later, every counterfeiter gets busted. And if you appreciate my work so much, why are you serving me this watered-down Ballantine crap?"

George laughed loudly. "We've got a lot of work to do tonight. No hard stuff until after dinner. We have to knock out all of the tens by the time we fall asleep tonight, and if you start talking to Mr. James Beam too early . . ."

"Alright, asshole," snarled Jimmy, "then let's eat dinner early. And if we're going to get everything done in time, let's open the barn doors so we can use more of the drying tables and get some air circulating."

"After I pull the steaks from the freezer to thaw, I'll open both doors slightly, and I'll set up all four tables. But if you see anyone come near the house make sure you close them in a hurry," said George.

George smiled as he walked back to the house. Jimmy was an artist. Anyone could shoot a negative, but watching how he worked for well over a week, sizing every intricate aspect of the bill and then adjusting the size and color of his projection of the word TEN overlaid on the Treasury seal demonstrated his true genius. Increasing and reducing the image size, brightening and darkening the image color . . . until it appeared perfect . . . the artist never rested.

But there was no way on earth that George could ever envision himself spending the rest of his life on a cramped sailboat with a psychopath like Jimmy Szymanski. He'd rather take the beer bottle opener to pry his eyes out from their sockets than be trapped with that crazy bastard for even a day on a boat at sea. Plus $60,000 in real cash could go a lot further with one person than $50,000 could for two.

As George went back into the house, Elbert noticed a vehicle entering the driveway from Annandale Road. The tow truck returning the old red pickup truck pulled its way around the gravel driveway, turning the corner and stopping just next to George's Ford Falcon. Elbert backed away from the bushes and stood behind a tree a few feet closer to the barn.

Hearing the tow truck pull forward, Elbert watched as Jimmy turned off the lights in the barn's office and closed the door, checking to make certain that it was locked. At the same time, George walked out from the house as the three men met in the driveway.

The tow truck driver lowered the truck from the bed while Jimmy and George approached with big smiles on their faces as phony as the ten-dollar bills they were printing in the barn.

As the men discussed the new engine that had been loaded into the truck along with a new clutch and complete brake and tire replacement, Elbert retreated quietly back into the woods, doubling back and forth over the creek before he arrived at the tree behind the barn. After climbing the tree, he dropped onto the roof of the barn from a pitch that couldn't be seen from the driveway.

While the three men discussed the torque of the new V-8 engine that Mancini had sprung for to restore the truck, Elbert quietly dropped through the vent to the ground below inside the barn. He had left the vent open from last time, and realized that it was a mistake for him to have done so, as it could have alerted Jimmy or George that they'd had a visitor. Depending on what happened this afternoon, he might have to double back, just to close the vent and cover his tracks.

Lying still on the ground below, he listened carefully to the men continuing to discuss repairs. To his left, under a wheel of the tractor, he again noticed the tail of the long black snake he had spotted on his earlier visit.

Moving as silently and rapidly as possible, Elbert got to the office door and gently turned the knob. As he'd hoped, neither Jimmy nor George had tested the door since he'd unlocked it on Sunday evening. He opened the door and crawled on his hands and knees to the back of the office, out of sight from the men in the driveway. He approached two tables in the back of the office. In a box on one rested bands of freshly printed $10 U.S. currency - counterfeit of course, but to his untrained eye, the bills looked as real as any he'd ever seen.

Elbert quickly grabbed one $10 bill each out of three of the bands, folded them, and placed them in the back pocket of his jeans. He grabbed an empty pint bottle of Jim Beam from underneath the table that Jimmy had likely tossed on the ground and placed it inside the waistband of his jeans. He crawled back towards the barn and closed the office door behind him. Then he heard the tow truck begin to pull away from the driveway.

"I'm glad we got the truck running again. I'm going to get back to work in the office," he heard Jimmy call out to George rather loudly.

"Good, I'll get to work on putting dinner together. I hope grilled rib-eyes with baked beans sound good to you?" asked George.

Elbert closed the inner office door behind him and moved towards the opening of the main barn door, where he waited to hear Jimmy enter the barn's office. Once he had, Elbert also listened for the sound of George entering the house, but couldn't be sure if he'd been distracted by the sound of Jimmy coming into the office.

Elbert calculated that his best chance to escape was to quickly slip out the barn door and exit around the right side of the barn, closest to the house, and then go behind the back of the barn into the woods and towards Jack's neighborhood.

The barn door was also still unlocked from when he undid it on Sunday. He wished he still had his cousin outside to let him know if it was safe to open the barn door and escape. He quietly pushed the door open just far enough to crawl outside. He then pressed it shut, stood, and turned to run around the right side of the structure. As he turned the corner to head towards the back of the barn, he was smothered in a solid, chest-high tackle from the 220-pound, solidly built body of George DiCandilo.

The impact of George's tackle was so solid that it took Elbert nearly thirty seconds to regain his breath, but it was the contact from George's stubby beard meeting Elbert's jaw that seemed to make him a little dizzy.

A few seconds later, Jimmy joined George, and waited until Elbert regained his ability to breathe. As he sat up, Elbert said, "I'm sorry, please don't tell my parents. I'll pay you for everything I've drank."

George kneeled on the ground, facing Elbert. "Why don't you tell us exactly what you've been up to son, and believe me when I tell you this, don't even think about trying to bullshit us."

Elbert learned from his father that whenever he spoke to adults, he needed to look at them straight in the face, right in their eyes, and to choose his words carefully. This advice applied especially at times when what he was about to say was absolute rubbish. So with his eyes fixed directly on George, Elbert straightened himself and removed the empty pint bottle from his jeans and said, "For a couple of days I've been sneaking through the woods and stealing some of your whiskey. I've only been able to grab two bottles, and the one I found today had less than a shot left in it, but the other day I nabbed one from the bannister on the porch that had about a third of the whiskey remaining."

George and Jimmy grilled Elbert on how he'd gotten into the barn. How many days had he been snooping around? What else had he been stealing? They slapped the pockets of his jeans but felt nothing, making them feel a little more comfortable that he had not taken anything important from the property.

"How old are you, kid?" George asked.

"I'm fifteen, sir," lied Elbert.

"I'm going to check around the barn to see if anything is missing," said Jimmy.

While Jimmy searched the office and looked around the barn, George eyed Elbert.

"You know, when I was fifteen years old, me and my friends would sneak into our neighbors' homes and borrow a little of their booze. But unlike you, I never got caught. I think I puked for three hours straight after stealing Old-Man Miller's scotch. That was my punishment," said George.

Elbert looked at George straight in the eyes and begged, "Please don't tell my parents. They have enough problems already, and the last thing they need is to have to bail me out of trouble. I can pay you twenty dollars within a week, just from mowing four lawns on Thursday and Friday. That should cover the whiskey I drank."

Jimmy completed his inspection and walked back to Elbert and George. "Everything looks okay," he said to George. "I saw the open vent on the roof where he came in. I need to talk to you about whether we should contact the police. But before we talk, we first need to keep him restrained. You wait here, and I'll tie him to a chair in the barn."

George reluctantly agreed and watched as Jimmy led Elbert to the barn. Inside, Jimmy sat him in an old bucket seat that had been removed from a Ford Mustang and was collecting dust and spider webs in a corner. He used clothesline to tie Elbert's hands and arms tightly behind him. He then tied the boy's feet together before tying his torso tightly to the chair. Next he dragged the seat to a post in the center of the barn, using more clothesline to tie Elbert's torso and neck to the seat and the post.

As he stood to leave, Jimmy slapped Elbert violently in the face with the back of his right hand. Elbert tasted blood in his mouth immediately and felt the heat from his cheek as it began to swell. Jimmy then wrapped duct tape around the lower portion of Elbert's head and mouth to prevent him from screaming for help. He added pieces of tape over Elbert's ears to muffle his hearing. Finally, he placed an old burlap bag over Elbert's head to keep him from seeing what they were up to inside of the office.

Chapter 25

Jimmy and George disagreed on what to do with Elbert. Jimmy believed that if they let him go, he'd probably tell his parents and they would likely call the cops to investigate. And if the kid had discovered that they were printing counterfeit notes, Jimmy and George would both be locked up.

George felt like the kid was just interested in the booze. He didn't want any trouble, and from what he could get out of the boy, he genuinely seemed more worried about his parents finding out what he'd been up to than what he or Jimmy had been working on in the office.

Jimmy Szymanski was the kind of person who liked to hurt weaker people he felt he could control. It gave him a sense of power in a world where he'd seen too many people look down their noses at him.

George DiCandilo, on the other hand, was the kind of person who liked to make the most amount of money while doing the least amount of work. But he didn't blame anyone for their shortcomings, and he certainly wasn't going to allow Jimmy to hurt a fifteen-year old kid who was just trying to steal some booze from their barn.

"Listen Jimmy," reasoned George, as he tried to remain calm. "You and I are counterfeiters. Counterfeiters are crooks who are sent away for up to twenty years if they get caught." He then pointed his stubby index finger, pressing it into Jimmy's chest, and said, "I'd rather be a convicted counterfeiter than an at-large murderer. We aren't hurting that kid. Do you have a problem with that?"

Jimmy could see that George wasn't playing around. If he challenged him, he knew that he'd need to be ready to pull his gun and shoot him. George had unusual strength for a man his age. The grip of his hand was normally gentle, but when he wanted to, he could instantly demonstrate his vice-like strength to make his point.

"OK. We will let the kid go. But let's do it right after we finish these batches of tens and finish with dinner. That will give me time to hide a few things in case the kid's parents do bring in the police," countered Jimmy.

George didn't want to escalate the tension between he and Jimmy any further. "Fine. As soon as dinner is over, the kid goes home."

Normally, during baseball practice, Jack tended to over-think every aspect of the game. "Was the line drive that Coach Russell hit to him in right field going to bounce off the turf before he could reach it, or should he make a dive for it? Should he swing for the fence on the first curve ball that he is thrown during batting practice, or should he just try to make contact? Was he concentrating on the pitch release to observe the spin of the ball, or was he thinking of other, non-relevant thoughts?" Some of these thoughts improved his concentration. Others often led to self-induced anxiety.

Today wasn't a normal day for Jack. His thoughts were on Elbert and his crazy idea to try to collect solid evidence on what Jimmy and George were doing at their house and in the barn. So when the line drive approached him in right field and he dove for it prematurely, he watched in utter shame as it bounced off the freshly mowed grass before him, hopping beyond his outstretched reach towards the fence.

Coach Russell withheld his verbal judgment until batting practice when he'd finally seen enough of Jack's overswinging at every pitch he threw. It was obvious to the Coach that Jack was not concentrating on the release, and it seemed as though his young slugger's only thought was how to swing harder and harder as each pitch came across the plate.

"Pull your head out of your ass! You're not concentrating, O'Malley!" shouted Coach.

Jack tried to pull it together during his last two swings, blasting two solid line drives to left field off of Coach's fastballs, but he had to agree that his mind was not focused on the field.

On the ride home from practice, Coach Russell asked Jack more calmly if anything was bothering him. Jack hesitated before answering and decided to use his father's four-week travel tour as his excuse. He promised his coach that he'd be back at 100% by game time and apologized for his distraction.

Pedaling the half mile or so from the Russell house to his own, Jack prayed as he rode up the slight hill into his cul-de-sac that he would find Elbert sitting in his front yard, grinning with the knowledge that his mission had been accomplished.

Chapter 26

Jack's prayers went unanswered. When he arrived home as dusk settled in on his neighborhood, he found no one in sight. He parked his bike at the end of the driveway and quickly ran into the house, only to find the home empty.

Dropping his glove on the dining room table, he stepped back outside his front door and listened for sounds. Sounds of voices, of laughter, or of movement in the surrounding homes. He could hear the radio blaring from Mr. Atkins backyard, and some laughter coming from the Allens' dining room, but instead he turned his attention to the Tucker home, where he quickly ran.

Jack spotted Brendan and Brian lying in Brian's front yard, testing each other's ability to name as many state capitals as they could. Jack reminded Brian that Jefferson City was the capital of Missouri, although, "St. Louis was a good guess."

"Have you guys seen Elbert, or do you know where Mom is?" asked Jack.

"Mom's at Mrs. Allen's house, helping her make curtains," said Brendan, "but I haven't seen Elbert in a while. And Mom told me to tell you that she left ham biscuits and buttered corn in the oven."

Jack said goodbye and ran to the Allen's house. He peeked in the front door and saw his mother and Mrs. Allen working at the dining room table, a sewing machine and fabric in front of them. Dana was sitting in a chair in the living room, but she stood and came to the door when she spotted Jack.

"What's up, Jack?" she asked as she slipped outside through the screen door. She could sense an urgency or impatience in him, even before he answered.

"Hi Dana, have you seen Elbert lately?" he asked.

"I haven't seen him all evening," she answered.

Jack turned to run towards his house.

"Jack, is everything alright?" asked Dana.

Without wanting to take the time to explain, Jack ran back home. Once inside, he grabbed a piece of notepaper and hurriedly jotted down a message. He folded it, and grabbed an envelope from his mother's small desk in the living room. He placed the note in the envelope and sealed it before running out the front door towards Mr. Atkins' yard.

Having heard the radio broadcast of the Senators' evening game coming from Mr. Atkins' backyard, Jack ran to join Mr. Atkins on his comfortable patio.

"What's the score, Mr. Atkins . . . I mean, Nelly?" asked Jack. He grabbed Mr. Atkins' coffee mug, adding, "I'll bet a Ballantine would taste great right about now. Don't you think?"

"Son-of-a-bitch. You scared the hell out of me," responded the truly surprised Nelly. "And ha - the score is zero-zero in the top of the second, and you are correct, Jackson O'Malley, a cold Ballantine would taste quite nice right about now. Ha!"

Jack returned quickly, carrying the mug of beer. He handed it to Mr. Atkins and held out the envelope he'd pulled from his pocket.

"Nelly, I am going into the woods to find my cousin Elbert, who has been exploring for a couple of hours," he said calmly. "If I'm not back by the top of the fourth inning, I want you to open this envelope and read the message that I wrote. And I hope you don't mind, but I borrowed about eight feet of the fishing line you keep in your shed.

And remember, please, don't open the note before the top of the fourth inning, please promise . . ."

Despite having numerous questions about what Jack was saying, Nelly nodded his head, taking the envelope as Jack headed off towards the woods. Why would Elbert be in the woods at this hour? And why did Jack need fishing line? Even more troubling, he wondered if this could have anything to do with the man with a gun who they had encountered? He sipped his beer and listened to the announcer call a strike from Camilo Pascual on the fifth pitch in the top of second inning. He tucked the envelope into his shirt pocket, cleared his throat with a heavy cough and whispered to himself, "Please be back here before the top of the fourth."

Jack, in the meanwhile, had run to the tree fort in the woods and climbed up the rope ladder. Searching under the tablecloth canopy he found the pellet rifle and the box of pellets. He removed a handful of pellets and tucked the rifle between his right arm and his torso and lowered himself from the tree.

He moved quickly over the creek and behind the bushes that he'd hidden in earlier in the morning. The light in the office was on, with Jimmy working hard at the printer. George worked in the back, invisible from where Jack crouched in the bush. Since the door to the office was open, Jack was able to overhear some of their conversation.

"I hope you're up for a long evening, Jimmy," growled George. "We still have a long way to go to knock out the tens this evening."

"Don't bug me, asshole," shouted Jimmy. "I'm moving as fast as I can. But with that little booze smuggler in the barn . . . I can only dry so many sheets at a time."

"I'm sorry, pal. I didn't mean to say you're moving slowly, but we need to let the kid go and tell him to never come back. My guess is that we'll never see him again. That way we can set up more drying tables in the barn," said George.

"I still don't trust him," said Jimmy. "If we let him go now, and he squeals to his parents, you and I are finished."

George walked towards the front door of the office and turned back to Jimmy. "You're right. But if we don't send him home soon, his parents will soon be calling the cops, and either way -- we'll be screwed. Plus, we agreed that once we were done with dinner, we'd let him go. And if I remember correctly, you finished every bite of your steak."

Jack had heard enough. He noticed that the lights in the barn appeared to be off from what he could see through the office windows. It wasn't his preference to take risks that he couldn't fully calculate, but he decided that he needed to act swiftly if he wanted to help his cousin and return home before Mr. Atkins opened the envelope.

Jimmy joined George on the front steps. George handed Jimmy the bottle of Jim Beam that he'd rested on the bench. George lifted a tumbler of the rye whiskey in a toast to his partner as Jimmy took a long guzzle from the bottle.

Shortly after their drink, Jimmy returned to the office with George while they printed and cut twenty more pages of the counterfeit ten-dollar notes. At the same time, Jack crawled beyond the bushes to a position where he was not visible from the front door or windows of the office. He then stood and ran behind the building to the tree that Elbert had used to climb into the barn.

Grabbing hold of the tree, Jack jumped to grasp a branch approximately seven feet from the ground. He'd used the fishing line he'd borrowed from Nelly to create a strap for the pellet gun. Jack placed the newly concocted, double-laced strap over his shoulder and pulled himself from one branch to another until his head was slightly above the barn's roof line.

Jack couldn't imagine how Elbert was able to climb the tree so easily. He stubbornly pulled himself past three additional branches until he stood above the roof. For Jack, inching his way up the tree line was a struggle, especially while gingerly trying to pinch the pellet gun between his right arm and his torso as he made his way, to minimize the strain he was putting on the fishing line strap.

Jack knew that he needed to drop into the barn to see if Elbert was there, even though he knew that he didn't have a plan in place if he was caught. He dropped to the tin roof from the branch above, using his left hand to grab hold of a roof seam while holding the pellet gun in his right hand to prevent it from banging against the roof.

Jack wondered to himself if the thud from his landing had alerted Jimmy and George of his arrival. This thought sounded an alarm throughout his nervous system as he lay quietly on the roof with his sneakers wedged into the tin roofline's vertical edges. His heart pounded so loudly that he had difficulty listening for sounds from within the barn or from within the barn's office, and a nervous sweat cut loose throughout his body.

Once his heartrate began to quiet, Jack looked upward to the vent that was now ajar, thanks to Elbert's handiwork. Calling on all of his might, Jack inched his way up the backside of the roofline until his left hand reached the open vent. Pulling his body closer to the vent, he soon felt both terror and amazement. Terrified that he was now clearly fifteen feet from the ground of the barn, and amazed at how easily his cousin reached and subsequently dropped from such a frightfully high location.

Jack again listened for any sounds or movements that might be coming from either the barn, the adjacent office, or from the driveway or the house. The only sound that consistently echoed up to the tin roof, however, was the steady hum of a machine that he assumed was the printer. That led him to believe that Jimmy was busy producing more counterfeit bills. But where was George? And was Elbert in the barn? Was he safe or was he injured, or even alive?

These thoughts motivated Jack in a manner that surprised even him. Looking inside of the barn through the vent opening, he was provided only brief glimpses of shadowy objects as what little light afforded by dusk began to disappear. He raised the pellet gun over his body and prepared to drop it to the floor, knowing that it would be impossible for him to drop from the ceiling while still holding onto the gun.

He aimed for an area that appeared to be free from machinery. Its bounce on the dirt floor below was impressive to watch and yet seemed to make only a minimal amount of noise. Hearing no subsequent sounds or movements from either Jimmy or George, he figured that they were still engrossed in their work in the office.

Jack placed his legs through the vent and grabbed the sides of the opening with both hands. He could hear a heated conversation taking place between Jimmy and George. The escalating volume of their voices provided the perfect background noise for him to lower himself and drop to the floor below. He prayed to land on solid ground and not on some piece of equipment, or even worse, on his cousin.

Chapter 27

Jack's feet touched the solid dirt floor and immediately his body crumpled to the ground with a thud. He lay still, listening for sounds from Jimmy or George. He felt his legs and arms and, to his amazement, all of his body parts remained intact and functioning.

"I don't care what you say!" shouted Jimmy at George. "If we let the kid go home, he is going to tell him parents that we held him as our prisoner, and before you know it, we'll have cops breathing up our asses. I don't want to kill the kid, but if we don't, you have to admit, all of our work here will have been a complete waste of time."

"Jimmy, for Christ's sake, listen to yourself!" shrieked George. "We are counterfeiters, not murderers." As he made this comment, he realized that Jimmy was already drunk, and that he'd completely forgotten about his promise to let the kid go home after dinner. He glanced at his partner's pistol, which Jimmy had shoved into his trousers, and concluded that Jimmy was going to kill the kid unless he stopped him.

"Listen, Jimmy," said George, eyeing the gun on Jimmy's waist, determining whether he could take it from him before he had time to react. "You're not a murderer. If we let the kid go home, he will probably tell his parents that he lost track of time while playing with his friends. But if you don't let him go, it's only a matter of hours, before police and bloodhounds are canvassing this area, and then what's your plan, you stupid son of a bitch?"

"The kid is a risk to our plans. I didn't invite him here. Hell, I even tried to scare him away when he came here with the little kid who looked like he'd pissed his pants when he saw my gun," said Jimmy. "I just don't see any option for us to let him go home to his parents, especially if he knows more than what he's telling us. The little bastard crawled through the roof of the barn for Christ's sake. Who knows what he saw?"

George stood quietly for a few moments. "I will only tell you one last time, Jimmy. If you hurt that kid, I'm done. I won't help you close the deal with Eddie. I'll just disappear, and you can finish this up on your own. I won't have a kid's murder on my conscience. So, what's it gonna be?"

Jack looked around the barn and spotted what appeared to be Elbert slumped in an old car seat in front of the tractor. Lowering his body, he crawled to his cousin in the darkness, hoping to move quietly and out of view from Jimmy and George in the office.

As he approached the chair, Jack raised himself onto his hands and knees and leaned into his cousin, whispering in his tape-covered ear, "It's OK, Elbert, I've got you covered from here." He watched Elbert's head raise as he sat up in the chair, despite the clothesline binding his hands and feet and the burlap bag shrouding his face.

Jack reached for his cousin's right calf and removed the knife from its leg-holster. He cut the strands of clothesline from Elbert's hands, allowing him to free his arms. Next he cut through the line that bound Elbert's waist to the chair, and the line binding his feet together.

Jack removed the bag from his cousin's head, and even in the poor lighting saw that Elbert's ears and mouth had been taped. He pulled the tape from his ears and unwrapped enough of it from his mouth to allow him to speak.

"Thank you, Jack," whispered Elbert.

Noticing the swelling around his cousin's mouth, Jack realized that he'd been beaten, and was about to tell Elbert that everything would be OK when the argument in the office grew in intensity.

"You're a psychopath," George yelled. "There was no way I was ever going on a boat with you!"

Then the struggle became physical. George pushed Jimmy into the office wall. This was followed by the sound and glare of two gun blasts ringing out. The sound of a body hitting the ground soon followed.

"Put the bag back on your head and act like you're still tied-up," whispered Jack.

Elbert did as his cousin instructed, while Jack quietly returned to the spot where he had dropped from the roof. Reaching around in the near darkness until he felt the cool frame of the pellet gun. He then slid to a position behind Elbert, hidden by one of the tractor's tires, just as Jimmy staggered through the office door, gun in hand, stumbling slightly as he came down the two short stairs to the floor of the barn. He staggered back to the wall near the office and flipped a switch that lit a bright lamp from the ceiling of the barn.

"You should have listened to me when I told you not to trespass," slurred Jimmy, as he staggered towards Elbert with the burlap bag pulled over his head. "You screwed things up, especially for my partner George. But I'll be damned if you're going to screw them up for me."

He stepped behind Elbert and began to raise the pistol from his side. But as Jimmy raised the gun towards Elbert's head, he suddenly fell to the ground as Jack struck the back of his skull with the butt of the pellet rifle. The sound of the strike felt so solid to Jack that it seemed as though he'd struck a melon with a baseball bat. As Jimmy's body fell unconscious to the dirt floor beside Elbert, Jack quickly grabbed the pistol and then pulled the burlap bag from his cousin's head.

"Let's tie him up and then call the police," said Jack as he hugged his cousin. "You have more courage than I'll ever have, but thanks for teaching me to grow some balls."

Jack opened the barn door and tossed the pistol into the bushes while Elbert dragged Jimmy's body to the car seat, securing him tightly with clothesline he found on the floor. He ripped a portion of the burlap bag and wrapped it around Jimmy's head at the mouth, knotting it tightly in his sweaty hair. When Jimmy regained consciousness and realized that he was now unable to move or speak, tears formed in his eyes, especially as he watched Jack empty the remaining portion of his fifth of Jim Beam, which he had discovered near George's lifeless, bullet-ridden body on the office floor.

Jack steadied himself on the handrail. His legs were shaking uncontrollably, and it took a few minutes for the tension in his muscles and nerves to relax and release. They were communicating a clear message to his brain. *Don't EVER do this to us again.*

As the trembling in his legs subsided, he watched his cousin pull the remainder of the burlap bag over Jimmy's head. Calming himself, Jack walked back into the barn and led his cousin outside, closing the door behind him.

Chapter 28

Fairfax County detectives Edward Carr and Bruce Dalton were the senior officers of the police force handling the crime scene. Detective Carr was probably about forty years old, but the lines on his face and his matter-of-fact demeanor made him appear ten years older. There was something about the way he handled himself in a crime scene that involved murder and counterfeiting that betrayed the fact that the detective had become too familiar with the corrupt side of life. He'd seen the lowest forms of human behavior long enough for it to begin taking its toll on his health.

Before Carr interviewed Elbert, he called in a forensics team and had the entire front of the house, the barn, and its office taped off. The forensics officers photographed the areas that had been cordoned off before lifting fingerprints from the office, barn, and home, along with the Ford Falcon and the truck in the driveway.

They collected Jimmy's handgun from the bushes where Jack had tossed it. They emptied the trash cans next to the house and placed the contents in police-evidence bags. The rookie officer collecting the trash was amazed to find fifteen empty Jim Beam bottles. Wasn't the trash collected weekly around here?

The forensics team and the ambulance squad examined George's body and then photographed him and the entire office before placing him in a body bag and loading him on a stretcher to be taken via ambulance to the county morgue.

While speaking with Detective Dalton, Jack observed the pathetic look on Jimmy's face as they removed the burlap bag from his head and cut the ropes from his hands, feet, and torso. He was then cuffed while the emergency medics bandaged the back of his head. Another officer read Jimmy his Miranda rights before placing him under arrest. Then three officers led him to a squad car and drove him to Fairfax County Police headquarters in Fairfax to be booked for murder and counterfeiting.

The emergency medics also looked at Elbert, cleaning the bruise on his face and giving him an ice pack for his cheek. They even examined Jack to make sure that he had no injuries.

The headlights from the police cruisers and other vehicles that were parked in the driveway shined so brightly that Jack and Elbert were unable to see if Jack's mother had arrived with Mr. and Mrs. Atkins. As the boys sat together in the back of a squad car, a man dressed in a dark suit and thin navy-and-red-striped tie leaned in through the front door.

"Boys," he said as he smiled. "My name is Jack Holtzman, and I'm an agent with the U.S. Secret Service counterfeit division. As soon as the county police are finished asking you questions, I'd like to honor your mother's request and take you boys back to your house so we can speak in the comfort of your home. Jack, I doubt you remember me, but I met you when you were about six or seven years old, when I sat in front of you and your dad at a Senators game. I was rooting for the home team, but I remember you wore a Yankees cap and did nothing but pull for the Yankees."

"I do recall that game, Agent Holtzman. You shared your peanuts with us, if I recall correctly. And yes, we'd be happy to speak with you when the police agree to send us home." He paused before adding, "And if I recall, sir, didn't the Yankees win that game, with Maris hitting a home run and Mantle adding two more?"

A few minutes later, Detective Carr told the boys that it was OK for them to go home and that he would probably stop by the next day to cover any follow-up questions that might arise. As he opened the car door to let the boys out, he looked down at them sternly from his 6'2" frame and said, "What you boys did here is remarkable. Stupid too! You both could have been killed. Do you know that?"

As Elbert exited the car, he looked at the detective with concern in his eyes. "It was all my fault, Detective Carr. I felt like we could get some evidence and safely call in the police before anything got out of hand. I'm from West Virginia, where we like to explore."

As Jack and Elbert walked back through the rows of law enforcement officers and the shining headlights of vehicles parked in the driveway, they joined Agent Holtzman and his partner, Agent Robert Powers, and were led towards their car.

"You might want to go say hello to those folks before we take you home," said Holtzman as he pointed to the crowd of people near Jack's mother.

Jack's eyes began to water as he saw the look of fear and anguish on his mother's face. Nelly and Dee Atkins stood next to her, along with Mrs. Allen and Dana. As Jack and Elbert headed towards them, Dana held her hands to her face as if she were holding a camera. With a huge smile on her face, she clicked a finger.

As Jack's mother embraced her son, she gasped for air, realizing that he was safe and in her arms. She then pulled in Elbert, embracing both boys together, letting the flow of tears wash down her face. "Thank God, you're both OK."

Nelly had been the one to call the police, and he looked knowingly at the boys as the others took turns embracing them. With his lips tightened, he nodded his head to Jack in a sign of pride in knowing that they had done something that went far above and beyond the call of normal civic duty. Now didn't seem like a good time for him to share with Jack that he'd read his note just five minutes after he had handed it to him.

As Dana hugged Jack, she whispered in his ear, "I just had to take a mental photograph, Jack. It's a moment I'll want to keep in my brain forever."

Chapter 29

Back at the O'Malley house, Agents Holtzman and Powers sat at the dining room table, while Mrs. O'Malley poured coffee. Elbert had spoken to his mother, who insisted on driving to Virginia tomorrow to stay with them for the next two weeks until it was time for Elbert to return home. Clearly upset, she would not be able to calm down until she could see her son and know that he was OK. Jack's dad had also called, from a hotel in Phoenix, Arizona, and though very proud of his son for saving his cousin, he was disappointed that Jack hadn't felt comfortable letting him know what he suspected was going on at that house. All things considered, the Secret Service was sending Jack Sr. home, not because Jack had embarrassed him, but because they wanted him to attend an award ceremony for Jack and Elbert for helping to bust a counterfeit ring that they'd been working on for the past four months.

Presently, Agent Holtzman stirred his coffee, pausing before he leaned across the table to speak. "I know you boys have already gone through this with Detectives Carr and Dalton, but we were hoping that you wouldn't mind reviewing everything with us, starting at the beginning."

Jack took his time, calmly reciting each segment of the saga. From building the tree fort in the woods, to Elbert and he nearly stepping on the copperhead snake, to Jimmy popping out of the woods with his threat and his gun. Elbert then joined into the conversation to discuss his nighttime visit to the house, the box with Crane embossed on its side. The trunk with packs of gum and cigarettes. The boys discussed how George and Jimmy enjoyed bourbon whiskey, often drinking a full fifth until they couldn't walk straight. They discussed Elbert's climb into the barn from the roof and how he could see that they had a printing press, but couldn't be sure of exactly what they were printing. Finally, Jack described what they had heard as George told Jimmy about the upcoming deal he'd arranged with two scary sounding guys named Fast Eddie and Dead-Eye.

"But we couldn't exactly hear when the deal was supposed to take place," Jack finished.

"Actually," paused Elbert, "I did hear George say that they were meeting at 8 p.m. this Thursday at the parking lot of Lake Barcroft."

While Elbert finished their tale, Jack shot his cousin a look that spoke volumes. He had always wondered why, from his vantage point in the tree, Elbert hadn't been able to hear more of the details of what George and Jimmy discussed that morning. Now he knew. Elbert must have understood that if he had told him those details, Jack would have insisted that they call the police immediately.

Agent Powers had been quiet during most of the meeting. Now he looked at Jack and asked, "So Jack, you didn't know that the exchange was supposed to go down on Thursday at Lake Barcroft?"

Jack paused before responding, trying to bury his initial feeling of betrayal. "You're very observant, Agent Powers. Elbert didn't tell me the time or place because he knew if he did, I probably would have insisted that we contact you then." He paused and then added, "But my cousin has always been able to think a couple of steps ahead of me. He knew that if we had contacted you then, you might have been able to capture Jimmy and George and even Mancini. But these guys would have all hired lawyers and your chances of ever nailing Eddie and Dead-Eye would have probably been shot." He smiled at his cousin and looked into Agent Powers' eyes. "Plus, Elbert knew that I was afraid of that guy Jimmy, and if for some reason you weren't able to convict him, he might very well have wanted to get revenge on me for ruining his $60,000 payday."

Agent Holtzman folded up his notebook and put his pen in his pocket, motioning to Agent Powers that it was time to leave. Before he turned away, Holtzman said, "You know, Elbert, you need to have a little more faith in the U.S. Secret Service. I'll be in touch with both of you tomorrow, but please do me a favor." Reaching out a hand and placing it on Jack's shoulder and then touching Elbert's non-swollen cheek, he said, "Other than talking with us, or with the Fairfax County detectives, or your parents, do not say anything about the Lake Barcroft meeting to anyone. If anyone talks to you about what happened tonight, leave out anything to do with the upcoming meeting. Got it?"

The boys nodded. "Yes, sir."

Chapter 30

Anthony Mancini had just returned from a fundraising dinner with his wife and was changing out of his tuxedo in his bedroom. His Golden Retriever, Sam, was barking repeatedly at someone knocking at the front door. Mancini shouted for Sydnee to answer, but when the barking continued he frustratingly trudged to the door wearing socks, black sweat pants, and a white tee shirt.

Special Agents Holtzman and Powers were accompanied by Detectives Carr and Dalton, along with four uniformed officers of the Fairfax County Police Department. By the time the team of law enforcement officers had gathered at Mancini's home at 11:15 p.m., they'd already determined that he was the owner of Mancini Printing and that his corporation also owned the house where George had been killed. They'd already obtained a signed statement from Jimmy that it was Tony Mancini, their former employer, who had provided them with the house in order to print counterfeit notes.

The police had also learned that for every $10,000 of cash George and Jimmy were able to bring in, Tony kept approximately $8,000, subtracting what he paid for the paper and ink and what he gave Jimmy and George in cash, food, and booze. Jimmy had already confessed to having helped pass nearly $600,000 in bogus money, primarily through drug dealers and pimps and through small purchases at a wide variety of convenience stores throughout the Washington metropolitan area, thus explaining the many packs of chewing gum and cigarettes that had been found in the trunk of the Ford Falcon. Even the registration of the newly refurbished pickup truck parked in the driveway was in Anthony Mancini's name.

As Sam growled and sniffed at the large contingent of law enforcement officers at the Mancini front door, Agent Holtzman bent down on one knee, calming the animal with one hand while showing his credentials to Mancini at the same time. He and Detective Carr instructed him that he was being arrested for aiding and abetting in the production and dissemination of counterfeit US currency. When they finished reading him his rights, Mancini insisted that they were making a mistake.

"Please, this must be some sort of colossal administrative error. I just returned from a dinner with several members of Congress and other dignitaries and believe me, once they find out what a blunder you are committing, you're all going to be sorry that you ever showed up at my door."

"Mr. Mancini, do you understand your rights that we have just read to you? If not, we will be happy to repeat them for you," said Detective Carr as he instructed two officers to begin a search of Mancini's home as permitted in their warrant.

Mancini's wife came to the door wearing a black, full-length nightgown. "Tony, what is this all about? I certainly hope that this won't impact my trip to Palm Beach this weekend with my sister."

Chagrined and subdued, Mancini looked at his wife and said, "Sydnee, just call Stephen Billings in the morning. He'll get this all straightened out. Just call my lawyer in the morning."

Sam stopped licking Agent Holtzman's hand as Mancini was handcuffed and led to the rear seat of the police cruiser in the driveway. Sydnee looked at her husband, with tears flowing down her face.

"Tony, What about my trip to Florida?"

* * *

Next Detectives Carr and Dalton scoured the house and the barn and recovered nearly $20,000 in real cash that Jimmy and George had earned from their activities and nearly $210,000 in counterfeit $10 bills. They also recovered the plates used by Jimmy to make the $20 bills, the Crane currency-standard paper, and ink tubes that were used in printing the black front face and green back of each bill, as well as other inks used to print the Treasury seal and the serial numbers on the bills.

Szymanski confessed to working with George on the counterfeit operation. He was the primary designer and printer, and George was the primary distributor of the bills. He spilled all of the facts surrounding their working agreement with Mancini, detailed their plans for Thursday's *"final transaction"* at Lake Barcroft, and provided background on the two noted criminals earning a living distributing drugs and supervising prostitution rings in DC and Baltimore.

He also confessed to shooting and killing George, but claimed it was in self-defense. He said that George slipped up during their argument, telling Jimmy of his plan to not give Mancini his cut from their final meeting with Dead-Eye and Eddie, and that he wasn't planning on giving Jimmy any of the extra $10,000 in cash, unless he gave him his gun and let Elbert go home. That admission was all it took to set Jimmy off on a tirade, but it was when George pushed Jimmy against the wall and went for his gun that Jimmy pointed the weapon at George and shot him. He claimed George was so much stronger than him that if it weren't for the gun, George would have killed him.

The prosecutor's office in Fairfax, therefore, was considering a plea arrangement with Jimmy in exchange for him joining in on the sting planned for Thursday, with an undercover Secret Service agent and a host of other Fairfax County police and Secret Service agents ready to help as needed. Jimmy knew he was going to jail, likely for the rest of his life, so the only thing on the bargaining table was whether or not he would be sent to a minimum security prison.

Chapter 31

On Thursday morning, the O'Malley family and Marcia Justice, who had arrived to both scold Elbert and shower him with kisses, headed off for a few hours of sightseeing in the nation's capital. Jack's Dad had scheduled tours of the Capitol and the Supreme Court. As a Secret Service Agent, Mr. O'Malley was also able to arrange a short private tour of the White House, including sections that were normally not on the public tour such as the Secret Service command post and the White House bowling alley.

At the Capitol, the family was led on a private tour by a Capitol intern who was a college sophomore from West Virginia University. Naturally, Elbert and Mrs. Justice were pleased to know that the Mountaineer state was well represented as they toured the House and Senate chambers. They even stopped into one of the Senate office buildings to visit West Virginia Senator Mason Randall, who was born just a few miles from Clarksburg. After welcoming the group into his private office, the Senator learned that the O'Malleys lived in Virginia.

"Well that's OK with me," he joked. "We're still hopeful that one day Virginians will see the light and secede to West Virginia!" He handed Elbert and his mother each a pen emblazoned with the crest of the U.S. Senate and asked them to visit him at his office back home whenever they were in Fairmont. "I want you to know, Elbert, that all of us in West Virginia are still mourning the loss of your father. He was a brilliant man and, frankly, one of the best human beings I ever had the pleasure to meet."

The family then took the short walk up First Street to the lofty marble stairs leading to the U.S. Supreme Court. They were led into the courtroom and seated along with a group of sixty or seventy others who were touring Washington from all parts of the country. A young woman entered the courtroom and provided the group with a broad history of the court, a description of the architecture of the building, a breakdown of which president appointed each of the current justices on the bench, and she explained the process in which cases were considered by the court, and more. Elbert especially appreciated that, of all of the buildings that they had toured, this was the first one where they were able to escape the hot sun and humidity for nearly thirty minutes and sit in an air-conditioned room without moving.

On the way home, Jack's father pulled into Angelo's Italian Deli in Arlington and picked up sandwiches and potato chips for everyone. Brendan had stayed back to compete in his first swim meet, and he greeted the family with the news that his team had finished in third out of four teams, while still clutching the 3rd place ribbon he'd earned from his individual freestyle event.

Dinner consisted of sub sandwiches, potato chips, and a salad, followed by homemade blueberry pie with vanilla ice cream. The entire extended family had the opportunity to hear Brendan describe his fifty-meter freestyle event in such detail that you would have thought he was a play-by-play announcer handling the call. Everyone told Brendan how proud they were of his performance in his first meet and Mrs. O'Malley even allowed him to have a second scoop of ice cream.

At 7:00 p.m., Jack and Elbert went outside and sat in the front yard while the grownups went out back for a cocktail with Dana's parents, who had come by to say hello to Marsha Justice. Jack and Elbert were sitting underneath an old oak tree that extended near their driveway, clearly with plenty of thoughts churning through their heads.

"You know, it was pretty cool how your dad kept our minds off of the sting operation that should be going down, in about an hour," said Elbert. "I can now say that I have visited the buildings that house the three branches of government for the most powerful nation in the world. I bet that less than one percent of the entire population in the U.S. has ever visited all three buildings, particularly in one day."

Jack nodded in agreement, though his concentration wasn't focused on their sightseeing. Jack was thinking about his parents. He felt that a big part of his father's qualms over his son not confiding in him about the operation in the woods was tied to his frustration that, in being an agent of the Secret Service, he was bound by a duty that forced him to forfeit his role as the daily protector of his family. An ironic observation for a person that presidential hopefuls relied on for their own personal security. Jack's mother seemed plagued by more practical worries. Had she not helped Mrs. Allen with her draperies the other night, could she have kept a better eye on Elbert and Jack and prevented them from traipsing into the woods on their dangerous expedition? Might they have told her what was going on and could she have alerted the police herself to get involved sooner?

"Until today, I hadn't ever been inside of the Capitol or the Supreme Court," Jack said as he returned his concentration to Elbert. "We'd driven by them before. A couple of years ago, we were invited to the White House around Christmas time, when President Johnson invited members of the Secret Service and their families to visit and get their pictures taken in front of a Christmas tree with the President. I remember how nervous my mom was that day, worrying about whether Brendan or I would misbehave. We have a picture of it somewhere."

After a minute of silence, Elbert smiled at Jack and said, "If you and I were to jump on your bike and Brendan's bike, there's a decent chance that we could make it to the Lake Barcroft parking lot just in time to witness the bust of Eddie and Dead-Eye."

Jack shot a look of near-disbelief at his cousin, realizing that he was kidding, but knowing that deep down, if he hadn't been warned by the police, the Secret Service, Uncle Jack, and especially by his mother, that Elbert would most assuredly have concocted a scheme to make his way to the parking lot to witness the activity, and to participate in its outcome in any manner that was necessary.

Elbert continued. "You know, Jack, I never actually thanked you for saving my life on Tuesday night. But I want you to know that for the rest of my life, I will owe you a debt that I may never be able to repay. If you hadn't clobbered Jimmy when you did," he paused, closing his eyes for a moment, "well, let's just say I don't think my mom could have dealt with another loss in such a short period of time."

He continued. "When I came here to visit, I was still hurting badly from Dad's death. You know, I really think that there were some suspicious circumstances surrounding his death. My dad worked on a lot of scientific stuff involving patents that could be worth millions of dollars to people, depending on who benefited from these discoveries. I have no evidence, no proof for my suspicions. Just a gut feeling. So, as I rode on the bus to visit, I guess my mind was still wrapped around the need to investigate, to learn more . . . to find justice. I may never be able to accomplish that with my dad, but with this little counterfeit ring . . . I don't know, maybe I felt like this was the next best thing."

"But without your action, climbing the tree, carrying the pellet gun, jumping into the barn from the roof and then nailing Jimmy as he came in to shoot me . . . If you ever had any doubts about coming through under pressure, I hope you'll remind yourself of that moment."

Dana had been sitting on the sidewalk in front of her house, and once she spotted Elbert and Jack under the oak, she scampered barefoot across the street to join them. She knelt in the grass next to Jack in her white jeans and a red tee-shirt, her blonde hair tied in a ponytail.

"Do you two mind if I join you?" she asked, and before anyone could answer, added, "I swear, Jack, today has been the most difficult day of my life. I've wanted to tell everybody about what happened last night, but my parents promised to send me to live with my Grandma in Danville if I said a word to anyone."

Jack smiled at her. "It's been a very strange day, for all of us. But with a little luck we should learn in an hour or two that the final act to this drama has concluded. And hopefully with a happy ending."

The three sat quietly for a few moments under the tree. From their position, they could hear their parents talking and laughing in the O'Malleys' backyard, the faint sounds of a Senators game blaring from Mr. Atkins' transistor radio, and nature's chorus, a symphony of crickets and katydids, as the light of another summer day faded into shades of night.

Unable to contain herself any longer, Dana stood and said, "Well, while you two sit here and wait around, I'm going to show you both how to hang upside down from a tree limb." Climbing the oak about seven feet from the ground, she crawled out onto a limb and dangled herself from the back of her knees. Her smiling face staring at Jack and Elbert, awaiting their comment.

"The monkeys at the zoo have nothing on you!" said Jack, as she grabbed the branch with two hands and flipped herself backwards, letting go at the last second to drop to her feet.

As 8:00 p.m. approached, Jack, Elbert, and Dana told their parents that they were going to visit the Atkins and listen to the ballgame. After all that had happened this week, Jack didn't want to make his parents worry if they couldn't find him and Elbert in the front yard. As soon as they walked into his backyard, Nelly rang out a loud, friendly welcome.

"Ha, my favorite people in the world!" Smoking a cigarette, Nelly took a final drag and extinguished the butt in his nearby ashtray. "And tonight, I see you brought my lovely next-door neighbor, Dana, to join us for the Senators game. Are you a fan of the Senators, like Jack?" he asked her as she found an empty lawn chair to join the group.

"You know, Nelly, from my room in our house, whenever my window is cracked open I can hear the Senators games from your radio, and although I couldn't name a single player on their team, something about hearing that broadcast of the game, along with the constant sound of the crickets at night, just feels like summer to me," she said. "And if I didn't hear your games from the radio each night, I'd feel like something was missing, so I guess what I am saying is, yes, I'm a fan, even if it's only to help me fall asleep at night."

"Ha, Ha, Haaa!" chortled Nelly. "I've always liked you Dana. You're as cute as a button, but you're tougher than most of the boys in this neighborhood. And I've seen you climb trees better than any of the boys, too. Scares the hell out of me to watch you! You need to go back to my shed and fetch three popsicles out of the freezer and bring them back here for you and your friends. And Jack, could you join her, and help me with a refill on my coffee mug, Ha?"

"Sure, Nelly," said Jack as he grabbed the coffee mug.

The Senators had scored two in the first and six in the second, all on singles, and now led the Indians eight to nothing heading into the third inning. As the group had settled in with popsicles and Ballentine, Nelly suggested Elbert knock on the screen door and ask Dee to come join them. As soon as she saw Elbert she lit up in a smile.

"Oh my, our hero from West Virginia has come to join us tonight. Let me give you a hug." She stood on her toes to reach around his torso. "You know we're all so proud of what you and Jack did on Tuesday evening. And the swelling on your face is completely gone."

Wearing a green floral-print dress, her hair pulled back into a ponytail and walking into the yard in her bare feet, Dee Atkins appeared to look twenty years younger than her husband, who had lit up another cigarette and taken a puff just as Jack handed him his mug and took his seat next to Dana.

"Well, Ms. Dana, it's a pleasure to have you join us with these fine young men this evening. Nelly, turn off that ballgame so we can hear ourselves speak," Dee commanded.

"Ha," laughed Nelly. "I'll have you know that Jack and his cousin are big-time fans of the Senators, and Dana here, she said that the sound of these games playing on my radio are what makes a summer evening feel perfect, and that it helps her fall asleep each night along with the sound of crickets."

"Hmmm," Dee replied. "Well, I just killed a cricket that had been making too much racket in the kitchen, and I have to agree with you, Dana, the sound of the Senators blaring on that radio puts me to sleep as well."

Dana laughed. She always loved the way Mr. and Mrs. Atkins could playfully banter with each other, and had watched how they helped care for each other with patience and concern over the years.

"Nelly," Dana asked after a time, "I've always wondered what your tattoos meant to you? I've been fascinated by those dice on your forearms."

"Ha," said Nelly as he took a sip from his coffee mug and set it aside on the table. "I haven't been asked about those tattoos in a long, long time. Most people are probably afraid to, maybe thinking that they represent something sad."

"Do they represent something sad? Because if they do, you don't need to say another word," said Dana.

"Ha," laughed Nelly, winking at Dee. "Quite the opposite my dear. These tattoos represent the two best days of my entire life. Ha, the two best by far! I got the first tattoo on June 3rd, 1937. I was a cocky young Sargent, stationed at Ft. Benning in Georgia, when I was ordered to attend a conference up in Atlanta for a few days."

"I think he actually spent more time visiting bars in Atlanta than he did attending his conference," interrupted Dee, a sweet smile emerging from her tight lips.

"Ha, well, there might be a little bit of truth to that, ha," said Nelly. "But anyway, one day while at the conference, I needed to mail a check to pay my utility bill, and as I was walking out of the post office, I saw an old Chevy coupe run right into the rear end of the Army Jeep that I had parked out front. I ran to check the damage, and found only a small dent in the bumper and a few scrapes on the paint. But the front panel of the Chevy had a long scrape and a snarled-up bumper. Ha, it looked like it had been bent in a vice."

"They don't want to hear every single detail, Nelly. Just get to the tattoo," pleaded Dee.

"Ha. I can tell that they are captivated by the details of this story," said Nelly, enjoying this opportunity. "So as I was saying, I stood for a few seconds checking on the damage, and out from the driver's seat pops the most beautiful young woman that I had ever laid eyes on. It turned out that she was a second-year law student at Emory, and the car she was 'trying' to drive belonged to her then-boyfriend, Archibald Winthrop Stevens, III, the son of Archibald Winthrop Stevens, Jr., who was the wealthy heir of an industrialist from Ohio."

"So this beautiful young law student, wearing a yellow sweater dress with black buttons and a black collar, and black shoes with yellow bows, looks at the vehicles and begins to tear up. Then she looks at me and says how terribly sorry she is."

Milking the story for every ounce of drama, Nelly added, "I wanted to diminish her obvious distress, to tell her that she didn't need to worry about the jeep, because it really didn't look that bad, but before I could open my mouth, Archibald Winthrop Stevens, III, jumps out from the passenger seat screeching, some sort of satanic scream that seemed to last for minutes."

"Stop calling him Archibald," said Dee, giggling. "You know he went by Archie."

Jack noticed the smile on Mrs. Atkins' face as she watched her husband telling a story she naturally knew, but with such dramatic detail that she couldn't resist hearing what new embellishment he might add.

Nelly continued. "So when he finally stopped screaming, he marched around the car and grabbed the young woman's arm and jerked her around and shouted *'How could you be so stupid! I never should have allowed a woman to drive the car that my Daddy gave me.'*

"But as he continued to add insult after insult I stepped between them and told him to calm down. 'There's no reason to get all worked up about a few dents and scratches,' I said." Nelly paused, winked at Dee, and took another sip from his mug. "But then Archibald

Winthrop Stevens decided to turn his anger towards me. He pushed me in my chest and said . . . now let me try to remember this word for word . . . *'Stay the hell out of this, you ignorant grunt.'* At which point, I introduced his forehead to the bumper of my jeep, for a closer inspection of the damage to the vehicle."

"Truth be told," interrupted Dee, "he may have introduced his forehead to the bumper a couple of times."

"Archibald," Nelly continued, "suddenly felt a little bit woozy, and needed to lie down in the seat of his Chevy. So, as he was attempting to regain consciousness, I walked back to the lovely and distressed young woman and introduced myself as Sargent Nelly Atkins. I said, 'Please don't worry at all about the jeep. I've dented a few of these vehicles a lot worse than this and if anyone asks what happened I'll tell them that I must have backed into a parking garage wall while I was here in Atlanta.'"

Dana interrupted. "Was Mrs. Atkins the beautiful young lady who wrecked your jeep?"

Both Dee and Nelly laughed out loud before Nelly simply continued. "Next, the beautiful young woman begins to tell me that she did not have a driver's license. In fact, most women didn't even drive in the late 1930s, but her boyfriend decided it would be fun to let her park the car when they got to the Post Office. But at that point, the woman corrected herself and said, *'He's really not my boyfriend, and after today, I don't think he and I will be spending any more time together.'"*

With his audience now fully captivated, Nelly sat back in his chair and took a long swig from his mug. "But then she said the words that I was really waiting to hear her say . . . *'Is there anything I can do to make up for this?'* Ha!" Nelly paused for effect. "At which point I said, 'There is absolutely nothing that you *have* to do to make up for this because accidents happen. But after meeting you here today, you would really make me happy if you would agree to have lunch with me tomorrow, so I can learn more about a young woman who is smart enough to be attending law school and who is courageous enough to drive a car without ever having taken a driving lesson.'"

"And it was Dee. Wasn't it, Nelly?" begged Dana.

"Yes it was, child. And it all happened on June 3rd, 1937 in Atlanta, Georgia. And I got the tattoo that evening because I knew I had met my future wife."

"And Dee . . . you agreed to go to lunch with him?" asked Dana.

"Oh Dana, I felt so sorry for the poor thing. He was begging so sadly. And believe it or not, he was pretty cute back then." She smiled at her husband as she answered.

"But what about the other June 3rd date on the other tattoo? You said there were two best days of your life, Nelly," said Dana.

"That's simple. On June 3rd, 1938, exactly one year later, that's when Deidre Anderson graduated from law school, in the morning. And married me in a beautiful ceremony in Atlanta, in the evening."

"If you can call a Justice of the Peace's 150-square-foot office, with your brother and my sister as witnesses, a beautiful ceremony," said Dee with a sly smile for all.

"So, Mrs. Atkins . . . sorry, I mean Dee . . . you graduated from Emory Law School? Did you ever practice law afterwards?" asked Jack.

Dee sighed. "You know Jack, by the time I'd finished law school I was already having second thoughts about whether I wanted to practice law. Nelly and I had moved back here when he was stationed at Ft. Belvoir, so I sat for and passed the bar exams in Virginia and DC, but let's just say that most law firms in the late 30s weren't eager to hire female attorneys. And like I said, I was having second thoughts on being a lawyer in the first place. I guess I always had an idealistic image of arguing important cases before the Supreme Court, you know, constitutional cases that could improve the lives of ordinary people. But a lot of my legal education focused on contracts, taxation, and criminal law that, frankly, bored me to death. So I applied for a job to teach in Fairfax County schools and taught government and civics classes off and on during Nelly's military career for twenty years before I retired."

"We visited the Supreme Court today. We learned about the process of how the justices are able to decide which cases they will agree to hear," said Jack.

"Your mother told us that she was taking you and Elbert on a sightseeing trip, but she didn't tell me that you were visiting the Court. Did you enjoy it?" Dee asked.

"Well, we were allowed to sit in an air-conditioned courtroom for a thirty-minute presentation. And after walking around a hot and humid city all day, I speak for myself when I say that I enjoyed it a lot," offered Elbert.

Everyone laughed.

"Well, Nelly, I think that the story behind your tattoos is beautiful, and every time I look at them I'll remember every word you told us. But Dee, when you said that you were married by a Justice of the Peace in Atlanta, with only your brother and sister as witnesses, does that mean that the rest of your family wasn't invited to the wedding?" asked Dana.

"Dana, that was very observant of you, but no, my family was all invited," answered Dee. "My mother and father didn't approve of my marriage because they didn't feel like Nelly was good enough for me. And Nelly's parents had both already passed away when he was just a child."

"Did your parents ever learn to accept Nelly?" asked Dana.

"Yes," Dee answered. "After Nelly returned from the war, my father and he sat out on my parents' patio for a couple of hours and talked about his experiences in France and in Germany. I think Daddy grew to appreciate the type of man Nelly was."

Nelly interrupted, "You may be right, Dee darling, but I think it may have had more to do with the whiskey that we drank on that patio . . . out of coffee mugs, if I recall correctly," he said smiling.

Chapter 32

At 8:01 pm, the red 1965 Mustang Fastback, packed with a 289 V8 engine and a four-speed Hurst competition shifter, slowly rolled through the entrance of the Lake Barcroft parking lot in Falls Church, VA. The car drove towards the Ford Falcon that was parked with its engine and lights turned off and then circled slowly once around the parking lot before pulling next to the Falcon.

William "Dead-Eye" Carter, age thirty-seven, sat behind the wheel of the Mustang. His passenger was his younger cousin, Allan "Fast Eddie" Monroe, age thirty-four. For both men, this was a business meeting. And in the seemingly affluent, albeit middle-class suburb of Falls Church, the lush green shrubs and trees surrounding the lake, with its small man-made sandy beach area nearby, only made Dead-Eye and Eddie more uncomfortable and tense that they had agreed to meet in an environment so foreign to the public housing projects of Washington and Baltimore, where they were accustomed to conducting their business.

They looked into the open passenger-side window of the Falcon and saw the smirk of Jimmy Szymanski staring back at them. Although the sunset had already fallen from sight, enough light remained for

Dead-Eye and Eddie to see that the driver of the vehicle was not their primary contact, George DiCandilo.

"Where is George, and who the hell's with you?" yelled Eddie to Jimmy.

"George needed to be rushed to Fairfax Hospital last night. Turned out the poor bastard had his appendix burst, so I needed to call an ambulance to get him in for surgery. He's not out of the woods yet. He has an infection and the doctors think he might have had a heart attack during the ordeal," responded Jimmy. "You know what he looked like. The fat bastard never ate a meal that wasn't either fried or filled with fat."

Eddie could sense that his cousin wasn't happy with the change in lineup, and quickly lifted his gun from his lap and pointed it across his cousin's chest towards Jimmy's window. "The last time we were together, I told you to not disrespect me, and here you bring in a complete stranger to a business meeting."

Jimmy had already been coached on this part of the engagement. He flashed his toothy smile at Eddie, his teeth stained from years of neglect, coffee, cigarettes, and booze. He held up his bullet-less pistol and said, "Fast Eddie, did I ever tell you that I can shoot a gnat's balls off from fifty yards with this thing? Put your damn gun back in your pants, unless you want to fire it."

Eddie slowly lowered his weapon.

"Since George wasn't around to help me finish with the printing and cutting," Jimmy said, "I needed to bring in our partner, Gus Andropolous, the man who owns the presses and supplies the paper and ink for us to work our magic." Glancing at Secret Service Agent Vincent Sporetti, Jimmy said, "Gus, say hello to Dead-Eye and Fast Eddie."

Gus nodded.

"We're not interested any longer," said Dead-Eye. "I don't like changes in plans, no matter what the reason."

"We understand," spoke Gus. "When George was taken into intensive care I tried to see if he could tell us how to get in touch with you so we could reschedule, but he's been unconscious since Tuesday night. I had to help Jimmy finish the printing job, and frankly we didn't have any free time to be driving around 14th Street to see if we could have someone direct us to Eddie."

"Big waste of time," said Dead-Eye as he fired up his engine.

"Just so you know, guys. I've got another buyer who will accept this deal as soon as I can set up the meeting. He's only willing to pay us ten cents on the dollar, but since you aren't moving forward, I want you to know that I have another customer who has needs," commented Jimmy, appearing smug as he spoke.

Dead-Eye cut off the engine. "Why would you be willing to sell your paper for ten cents a bill, when you wanted us to pay you twelve?"

Gus spoke up again. "Listen guys, we can't risk flooding the area with more than half a million dollars-worth of bills at one time. Once we do a deal this size in this region, we're going to have to relocate to Chicago or Detroit, to spread out our distribution. You guys are understandably concerned about the absence of George, so you prefer to pass. We get it. So our next best option is to deal with a fat Italian prick, who's only willing to cough up ten cents per bill – but for now, he's our best prospect for such a large amount."

Dead-Eye held up his index finger, motioning Jimmy and Gus to sit tight. He told them to give them ten minutes and asked what George's last name was. After Gus provided him with the name, Dead-Eye drove to a corner 7-Eleven and from a pay phone asked the operator to connect him to Fairfax Hospital. When he was connected he asked the operator to put him through to the Intensive Care Unit and then asked the attendant if he could possibly speak with his uncle, George DiCandilo.

"I'm sorry sir, but your uncle is still unconscious and cannot speak to you at this time. But we are hopeful that he'll regain consciousness by morning."

Dead-Eye hung up the phone convinced that Jimmy's story about George must be true, unaware that a Fairfax County police technician was handling the Intensive Care's switchboard for the evening. Returning to the parking lot at the lake, Dead-Eye again pulled next to the Falcon and rolled down the window.

"If you'll give us the same deal as your Italian friends, ten cents per dollar, we're ready to do business."

Gus held up his index finger, requesting a conference with Jimmy as he rolled up the window to the Falcon. Gus appeared to be pleading with Jimmy, while Jimmy appeared upset and agitated. After a few additional exchanges, Jimmy rolled down the window, and with a very unpleasant look on his face said, "Dead-Eye, you've got a deal. $50k for $500k in tens and twenties."

Gus turned on the headlights of the Falcon, and said, "Let's bring everything out in front of the car so we can make sure everything is in order."

Eddie and Dead-Eye exited the car with Dead-Eye carrying a brown grocery bag, rolled up at the end, to form a handle. Gus popped the trunk of the Falcon and carried two boxes of bills, with one containing 25,000 ten-dollar notes and the other containing 12,500 twenty-dollar bills. He dropped them in front of the grille of the Falcon so they could be inspected in the headlights.

"You're getting a hell of a deal. Those are the finest twenty-dollar bills ever printed," moaned Jimmy. "I created 12,500 different serial numbers for Christ's sake. You could pass these things at the Federal Reserve and you'd never be questioned."

Dead-Eye focused on the twenties. Looking at the serial numbers he could see that, in fact, the serial numbers didn't match. He held one to his nose and remarked, "They even smell like the real thing."

Gus counted out the $50,000 in cash that Dead-Eye had handed them in the grocery bag. "Gentleman – it's been a pleasure doing business with you. Be careful with that money."

As they turned to return to their car, Eddie kept his gun pointed at Jimmy. "Let's take them out here, I want to keep their bills and our cash."

Gus paused before opening the door to climb in. "Eddie, I hope you haven't underestimated us that badly. We've already left a message letting it be known exactly who we are meeting with, where you live, your line of work, and exactly what you have in your possession. If we don't return and destroy that message before ten this evening . . . Let's just say that you'll both have so many Feds climbing the streets of DC and Baltimore that you'll need to relocate to Argentina."

Dead-Eye shot a look at Eddie as he climbed into the Mustang, and Eddie followed suit. The Falcon pulled out of the lot and turned off its lights as it turned the corner and disappeared from sight. As Dead-Eye put his car into gear, he noticed headlights entering the park followed by vehicles with sirens and flashing lights.

"It's a set-up!" shouted Dead-Eye to his cousin.

He circled the lot looking for any possible exit before finally driving his Mustang through bushes and onto the hundred-yard beachfront facing the lake. Opening the car door, spotlights seemed to be flashing at him from all directions.

"William Carter, Allen Monroe," a voice addressed them through a megaphone, "you are under arrest. Throw down your weapons onto the sand and lie face down with your hands behind your head."

The spotlight from a helicopter above moved closer to the beach. Police officers carrying rifles and flashlights and dressed in dark outfits approached from all directions. Dead-Eye tossed his pistol into the sand and lay on the ground, face down as instructed, but Eddie made the mistake of ignoring the instructions and aimed his weapon at the helicopter. He fell immediately as a sniper shot pierced an inch-wide hole in the center of his forehead. A steady flow of blood drained into the white sandy beach as his lifeless body stared open-eyed towards his cousin.

Chapter 33

Later that night Jack and Elbert were called away from the Atkins'
yard to meet with the detectives back home. They entered the living
room to find a whirlwind of activity before them. Detectives Carr
and Dalton were accompanied by Agents Holtzman and Powers and
none other than Fairfax County Police Chief Nelson Albright. Jack's
dad took charge and asked everyone to have a seat.

"I know that everyone has already met, but Chief Albright, let
me introduce you to my son Jack and my nephew Elbert Justice."

The boys stood and shook hands with the Chief and returned to
their positions on the living room sofa.

"Boys," Mr. O'Malley continued, "the Chief is here to tell you
about the events that took place this evening at Lake Barcroft and to
ask you to attend a special ceremony tomorrow morning."

The chief thanked the boys for their acts of courage and in
assisting the police department and the U.S. Secret Service in
apprehending a counterfeiting ring that had been inflicting financial
pain throughout the DC metropolitan area for nearly a year. Until
Tuesday, he admitted, his police force had been unable to connect
the counterfeit bills to any solid suspects.

The chief then described the Lake Barcroft sting operation as a joint venture, between his police department and the Secret Service. Szymanski had agreed to serve whatever sentence he ended up with in a low-to-medium-level security prison, pending the filing of additional charges of attempted murder of Elbert. He announced that the sting had turned out exactly how they had drawn it up, though unfortunately Fast Eddie was shot and killed during the operation. Dead-Eye, with his rap sheet for drug distribution and prostitution, didn't stand a chance of being released on bail.

"In all my 39 years on the police force, I've never seen a case like this. Particularly one that was brought to us by a twelve- and thirteen-year-old. Boys, we owe you our gratitude for helping us with these arrests, although we would have preferred to have been notified as soon as you knew what they were up to. What you both did took a lot of courage and we all want to say thank you," said the Chief.

As the room quieted, Jack asked, "I was wondering, Chief Albright, since Jimmy and George hadn't finished making all of the ten-dollar bills and hadn't even started on the twenties, how did Jimmy and the undercover agent make them believe they were getting the full $500,000?"

The Chief glanced at Agents Holtzman and Powers and said, "Good question, Jack, but I think I'll leave this one to the Secret Service to answer."

Agent Powers stood. "Jack, as I'm pretty sure you know, the Secret Service is a part of the Treasury Department. But did you know that the Bureau of Engraving and Printing is also a part of the Treasury? We went to our boss, and our boss's boss, who then went to the Director of the Secret Service, who likely ended up talking to the Secretary of the Treasury. Eventually, we obtained 12,500 twenties and about 1,000 tens from the Bureau of Engraving and Printing. As it turns out, whenever the Bureau of Engraving produces a batch of bills with even the slightest flaw, the bills are pulled from circulation and destroyed, and it just so happened that they had a few batches of these corrupted bills that were about to be destroyed before we borrowed them. So in actuality, we handed Eddie and Dead-Eye

$240,000 in counterfeit bills and $260,000 in *nearly* legal tender in exchange for the $50,000 that they paid during the sting."

Agent Holtzman added, "And thank God, we were able to make sure that every one of those nearly real bills was returned tonight, or else Agent Powers and I would have been transferred to Anchorage, Alaska for the remainder of our careers!"

* * *

The following morning Jack headed out before sunrise to complete his daily workout and run. When he returned to the house, his father was in the kitchen, preparing a pot of coffee.

"You're up early, Jackson."

"Got my workout knocked out early," Jack replied, handing his father the morning paper.

"Jack, since it's just you and me here in the kitchen, there's something I wanted to ask you," said Mr. O'Malley as he poured milk into his mug of coffee. "Now that the bad guys are either dead or in jail, I'd like to know what you have learned from this experience."

Mr. O'Malley motioned his son to join him at the dining room table, where they both took a seat. Jack wiped sweat from his forehead as he considered his words.

"I'm happy that Jimmy, Mancini, and Dead-Eye are going to jail for what they have done. But to be involved in an activity where two people were killed is . . . well, it's beyond my ability to completely explain." Jack paused. "You know, Dad, for most of my life, I've always been afraid. Afraid of embarrassing myself. Afraid of screwing up. And guess what? During all those years of being afraid of making a mistake, I trained myself to avoid risk at any cost. But I never felt proud of myself. Mostly I felt ashamed."

Jack looked at his father squarely in the eyes and explained, "But being able to hang out with Elbert . . . It just showed me that sometimes, if you're afraid and let your fears get the better of you, worse things can happen. So when I felt that Elbert's life was at stake I somehow reacted without thinking, doing what my instincts told me not to do. I'm really not sure if I was angry or scared about what Jimmy wanted to do with Elbert, but somehow it motivated me to act. And you know Dad . . . I don't feel ashamed of myself. I feel proud. Maybe prouder than I've ever felt in my life."

Jack's father rubbed his son's brown sweaty hair, pulled his bangs from his eyelids, and said, "Son, I think you learned a pretty valuable lesson from this experience. Sometimes having a fear is a good thing. Lord knows I have fears from time to time. Fears can protect you from things you weren't prepared to handle by signaling you to use caution. But knowing when to stand up to your fear and when to avoid the risk . . . that comes from experience, from using judgement to determine what the consequences will be if you take action or if you don't. But one thing is for sure, in the future, when the pressure is on and the stakes are high, now you'll know that you have what it takes to deliver."

At 8:00 a.m., the O'Malley household, Justices included, crammed into the family station wagon and drove to the house in the woods. Mr. O'Malley could barely pull the car into the driveway due to the number of police, Secret Service, newspaper, and television vehicles that had appeared for Chief Albright's press conference.

A podium with the insignia of the Fairfax County Police department had been placed, attached with microphones from all of the local television and radio news stations, upon a temporary stage that had been pieced together in front of the barn in the driveway. More than eighty credentialed news reporters, cameramen, and photographers stood as members of the Secret Service and the Fairfax County Police Department stood behind the chief, who called the media to order.

Jack, Elbert, and their families stood near the front porch of the house and watched the press conference begin. Elbert wore one of Uncle Jack's white button-down dress shirts, which fit him pretty well even though the sleeves were a little short, along with a pair of blue jeans and black loafers that his uncle had also loaned him. Jack wore a light blue button-down with grey slacks and a pair of burgundy penny loafers, just like he might have worn to church, only this time without a tie or navy sportscoat.

Chief Albright took control of the audience, introducing Detectives Carr and Dalton and Special Agents Holtzman and Powers. He succinctly described the arrests and charges against Jimmy Szymanski, Anthony Mancini, and William "Dead-Eye" Carter as well as the deaths of George DiCandilo and Allen "Fast Eddie" Monroe. He announced that the detectives and the Special Agents would not be available for questions afterwards due to the ongoing investigation and criminal proceedings.

Albright next introduced Jack and Elbert. By this time, Jack had noticed many of his neighbors had traipsed through the woods to view the media circus. Gary and Brian were watching intently, and Dana stood with her mother next to Nelly and Dee Atkins, who had somehow managed their way down the hill, through the woods, and over the creek to stand near the very same ferns where Jack had once hidden.

Jack and Elbert walked nervously in front of the stage and faced the crowd as cameras clicked and tape rolled. Elbert had a steady tight-lipped smile on his face while Jack grinned broadly, especially after glancing at Dana, who had her fingers in front of her face once more, taking her own mental photograph of the occasion.

While the boys remained in front, Chief Albright explained more details of the counterfeit operation and thanked the joint efforts of the US Secret Service and the Fairfax County Police Department, specifically recognizing Agents Holtzman and Powers and Detectives Carr and Dalton for their efforts. The chief then described the roles that Elbert and Jack played in bringing this entire operation to its conclusion: Elbert's attempt to collect evidence, his capture, and Jack's rescue just as Szymanski was attempting to shoot and eliminate Elbert as a witness.

"Let me be very clear," continued Chief Albright, "we would have preferred that Elbert and Jack had notified us much earlier in the process, as soon as they suspected that something inappropriate was occurring on this property, as this could have allowed us to begin our work sooner and protect them from the type of harm that they both faced." He paused. "But regardless of their notification timing, on behalf of the Fairfax County Police Department, and I believe I can speak for our partners at the U.S. Secret Service and for all citizens in the DC metropolitan and Baltimore metropolitan areas that were about to be encumbered by another half a million dollars of counterfeit money, we owe you both a tremendous amount of thanks for your courage and your resourcefulness, in preventing these criminals from perpetrating further havoc upon our communities."

The law enforcement officials, the media who had their hands free, and the friends and family in attendance all applauded as more photographs were snapped of the two unlikely heroes.

As the press conference concluded, Gary Saunders lobbied unsuccessfully to find a single reporter willing to provide even a mention of his name or a reference to his tree fort in their coverage. With his head shaking in disappointment, he yelled in exasperation to the exiting reporters, "Without my fort, none of this would ever have happened."

That afternoon, at a later ceremony at Secret Service headquarters in Washington, Jack and Elbert were presented with a plaque for service above and beyond the call of duty from Director Daniel Crawley. In the photograph of the ceremony with Jack and Elbert were agents Holtzman, Powers, and John "Jack" O'Malley.

Chapter 34

On Saturday morning at nine, Jack's father loaded the family into the car and drove the two-mile distance to the Annandale Recreational Park for the league championship game between the two teams tied for first place in the division: the Cardinals and the Pirates. On Annandale Road, as they rode past the entrance to the house and the barn where so much had happened in the preceding days, Jack and Elbert stared intently and then looked at one another and smiled quietly.

For some unknown reason, Elbert felt tears welling in his eyes. He was suddenly overcome with intense emotion, and shuddered. He had nearly gotten himself killed. And Jack had to risk his life to save his. But his thoughts settled down as he focused on how he wished his dad could have been with them yesterday, concluding that maybe, at least in spirit, he was with him, even now.

Jack sensed his cousin's emotions but quickly looked away to avoid making Elbert feel uncomfortable. He'd hoped their time together, especially their adventures in the woods at the barn, had been both a distraction and a relief to his cousin, who had suffered a loss that was bigger than any he could imagine. Elbert had been his role model, showing him what he could accomplish if he didn't allow fear to overwhelm him. It had taken him awhile, and maybe it had required his cousin's life being in danger, but somehow he had mustered the strength to act more like the role model that Elbert had become.

The front-page story in yesterday's *Evening Star*, the televised broadcast of Chief Albright's press conference, and this morning's *Washington Post* article had made Jack and Elbert momentary celebrities to the other players and their parents at the ballpark. Several stopped and stared at the boys as they arrived. A few even shouted out, "Way to go, boys!"

As Jack approached the diamond on his way to the Pirates dugout, Elbert grabbed his elbow and motioned him to join him a few steps away. Elbert cupped his hands around Jack's ear.

"If you face that big guy today, who looks likes like he's growing a beard," he said, "I saw him do two things for you to keep in mind . . ."

As the game approached the bottom half of the final inning, the Pirates came to bat knowing that they needed at least one run to tie the game and two to win. Jack had enjoyed a great game at the plate, with a single and a double, both knocking in runs. And he had scored himself, when a throwing error to third allowed him to slide into home safely in the fourth inning. But the Cardinals always seemed to be able to do just enough to keep ahead of Jack's team and they led the game five to four.

Allen Tallman had started for the Cardinals and, as usual, had proven to be a very solid pitcher. He'd only given up five hits and two walks and had stuck out nine Pirates through five innings.

When Tallman walked Randy Russell to lead off the bottom of the sixth inning, Jack wasn't the least bit surprised when he saw Cardinals Coach Dunnington head out to the mound and bring in his son, Bobby, from left field to replace Tallman. Jack backed away from the on-deck circle as Coach Russell approached, reminding him, "Look at the release of the ball, Jack. Focus on the release and knock the cover off the ball."

Jack took a knee as Dunnington threw a few final warm-up pitches, but focused intently on every gesture the pitcher made as he gripped the ball, and observed how each pitch entered the catcher's mitt.

As play resumed, Jack nodded towards the pitcher and stared at his throwing hand, which he hid in his mitt in front of his face. Noticing little movement of the pitcher's throwing hand, Jack anticipated a fastball, which he indeed received, but Dunnington overthrew it and it went high and slightly outside for ball one.

Prior to the second pitch, Jack noticed Dunnington working the ball in his glove, which, based on Elbert's advice, alerted him to expect his curve. Jack focused on the pitcher's release and saw the ball appear to rise towards his head, but by betting on the curve he delayed his swing for an extra moment before watching the pitch drop towards his waist on the inside corner of the plate. Jack struck the ball hard, but a little late, fouling it over the Cardinals dugout and above the bleachers beyond.

With a one and one count, Jack watched Dunnington prepare for his next pitch and again observed his right hand working to obtain the proper grasp of the seams. Expecting a curve again, Jack zeroed his focus on the release of the ball and again watched as it appeared to head towards his shoulder. But unlike his earlier pitch, this pitch hung at his chest and crossed the middle of the plate . . . until it met with the head of Jack's Louisville Slugger. There was a thunderous crack. The moment the ball left his bat, Jack never had any doubt about where the ball would land, or which team had won the game.

As he rounded third base and approached home, he glanced into the stands and smiled as his family and friends stood, screaming and cheering. He glanced at the pitcher, who looked at him, his face etched in disappointment as he turned and walked towards his dugout.

As Jack touched home plate, mobbed with teammates celebrating all around him, he glanced again into the stands to see his father, mother, aunt, cousin, and brother, all wearing huge smiles. Nelly and Dee Atkins were high-fiving every fan within reach. And Dana stood clapping, smiling, and staring right at him.

Jack returned her smile, formed an imaginary camera with his fingers, and took a mental photograph of Dana, with his family.

Printed and bound by PG in the USA

USA2019PGIL